D1020671

The dragon coiled around Byron.

THE SPIDERWICK CHRONICLES

THE WRATH OF MULGARATH
BOOK FIVE OF FIVE

Tony DiTerlizzi *and* Holly Black

SCHOLASTIC INC.

New York   Toronto   London   Auckland   Sydney
Mexico City   New Delhi   Hong Kong   Buenos Aires

ISBN 0-439-73568-8

12 11 10 9 8 7 6 5 4 3 2 1   5 6 7 8 9 10/0

Printed in the U.S.A.   23

First Scholastic printing, January 2005

Book design by Tony DiTerlizzi and Dan Potash

For my grandmother, Melvina,
who said I should write a book just like this one
and to whom I replied that I never would
—H. B.

For Arthur Rackham,
may you continue to inspire others
as you have me
—T. D.

Table of Contents

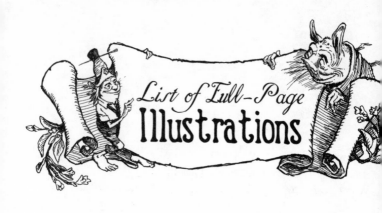

List of Full-Page Illustrations

Dear Reader,

Over the years that Tony and I have been friends, we've shared the same childhood fascination with faeries. We did not realize the importance of that bond or how it might be tested.

One day Tony and I—along with several other authors—were doing a signing at a large bookstore. When the signing was over, we lingered, helping to stack books and chatting, until a clerk approached us. He said that there had been a letter left for us. When I inquired which one of us, we were surprised by his answer.

"Both of you," he said.

The letter was exactly as reproduced on the following page. Tony spent a long time just staring at the photocopy that came with it. Then, in a hushed voice, he wondered aloud about the remainder of the manuscript. We hurriedly wrote a note, tucked it back into the envelope, and asked the clerk to deliver it to the Grace children.

Not long after, a package arrived on my doorstep, bound in red ribbon. A few days after that, three children rang the bell and told me this story.

What has happened since is hard to describe. Tony and I have been plunged into a world we never quite believed in. We now see that faeries are far more than childhood stories. There is an invisible world around us and we hope that you, dear reader, will open your eyes to it.

HOLLY BLACK

Dear Mrs. Black and Mr. DiTerlizzi:

I know that a lot of people don't believe in faeries, but I do and I think that you do too. After I read your books, I told my brothers about you and we decided to write. We know about real faeries. In fact, we know a lot about them.

The page attached* to this one is a photocopy from an old book we found in our attic. It isn't a great copy because we had some trouble with the copier. The book tells people how to identify faeries and how to protect themselves. Can you please give this book to your publisher? If you can, please put a letter in this envelope and give it back to the store. We will find a way to send the book. The normal mail is too dangerous.

We just want people to know about this. The stuff that has happened to us could happen to anyone.

Sincerely,

Mallory, Jared, and Simon Grace

*Not included.

At the gate of the Spiderwick estate

Chapter One

IN WHICH the World Is Turned Upside Down

The pale light of the newly risen sun made the dew shimmer on the nearby grass as Jared, Mallory, and Simon trudged along the early morning roads. They were tired, but the need to get home kept them going. Mallory shivered in her thin white dress, clutching her sword so hard that her knuckles went white. Beside her, Simon shuffled along, kicking stray bits of asphalt. Jared was quiet too. Each time his eyes closed, even for a moment, all he saw were goblins—hundreds of goblins, with Mulgarath at their head.

Jared tried to distract himself by planning what he would say to his mother when they finally got home. She was going to be furious with them for being gone all night and even madder at Jared because of that thing with the knife. But he could explain everything now. He imagined telling her about the shape-shifting ogre, the rescue of Mallory from the dwarves, and the way they had tricked the elves. His mother would look at the sword and she would have to believe them. And then she would forgive Jared for everything.

A sharp sound, like a tea kettle whistling at full volume, snapped him back to the present. They were at the gate of the Spiderwick estate. To Jared's horror, trash, papers, feathers, and broken furniture littered the lawn.

"What is all that?" Mallory gasped.

A screech drew Jared's eyes upward, where

Simon's griffin was chasing a small creature around the roof and knocking pieces of slate loose. Stray feathers drifted over the roof tiles.

"Byron!" Simon called, but the griffin either didn't hear or chose to ignore him. Simon turned to Jared in exasperation. "He shouldn't be up there. His wing is still hurt."

"What's he after?" Mallory asked, squinting.

"A goblin, I think," said Jared slowly. The memory of teeth and claws red with blood awakened a horrible dread within him.

"Mom!" Mallory gasped, and began to run toward the house.

Jared and Simon raced after her. Up close they could see that the windows of the old estate were smashed and the front door hung by a single hinge.

They darted inside, through the mudroom, stepping over scattered keys and torn coats. In the kitchen, water poured from the faucet, filling a sink piled with broken plates and spilling onto the floor, where food from the overturned freezer was defrosting in wet piles. The wallboard had been punched open in places, and plaster dust, mingling with spilled flour and cereal, covered the stove.

The dining room table was still upright, but several of the chairs were knocked over, their caning ripped. One of their great-uncle's paintings was slashed and the frame was cracked, although it still hung on the wall.

The living room was worse: The television was shattered and their game console had been shoved through it. The sofas were ripped open, and stuffing was scattered across the floorboards like drifts of snow. And there, sitting on the remains of a brocade footstool, was Thimbletack.

"All my fault, all my fault."

As Jared moved closer to the little brownie, he could see that Thimbletack had a long, raw scratch on his shoulder and that his hat was missing. He blinked up at Jared with wet, black eyes.

"All my fault, all my fault," Thimbletack said. "I tried to fight; my magic's too slight." A tear rolled down his thin cheek, and he wiped it away angrily. "Goblins alone I might have driven off. The ogre just looked at me and scoffed."

"Where's Mom?" Jared demanded. He could feel himself trembling.

"Just before the break of day, they bound her and carried her away," Thimbletack said.

"They *can't* have!" Simon's voice was close to a squeak. "Mom!" he called, rushing to the stairs and shouting up to the next landing. *"Mom!"*

"We have to do something," said Mallory.

"We *saw* her," Jared said softly, sitting down on the ruined couch. He felt light-headed, and hot and cold at the same time. "At the quarry. She was the adult the goblins had with them. Mulgarath had her, and we didn't even notice. We should have listened—*I* should have listened. I never should have opened Uncle Arthur's stupid book."

The brownie shook his head vigorously. "To protect the house and those inside is *my* duty, Guide or no Guide."

"But if I had destroyed it like you said, none of this would have happened!" Jared punched himself in the leg.

Thimbletack scrubbed his eyes with the heel of

his hand. "No one knows if that is true or not. I hid it away—see what we got?"

"Enough with the pity party—neither of you is helping!" Mallory squatted beside the footstool, handing the brownie his hat. "Where would they have taken Mom?"

Thimbletack shook his head sadly. "Goblins are filthy things, the master worse than his hirelings. They would dwell somewhere as foul as they, but where that is, I cannot say."

From above them there was a whistle and a clatter.

"One goblin is still on the roof," said Simon, looking up. "It must know!"

Jared stood up. "We'd better stop Byron before he eats it."

"Right," said Simon, heading up the stairs.

The three kids ran up the steps and down the hall toward the attic. The bedroom doors on the second floor were open. Torn clothing, pillow feathers, and ripped bedding spilled out into the hall. Outside Jared and Simon's shared room, cracked, empty tanks lay on the floor. Simon froze, a stricken expression on his face.

"Lemondrop?" Simon called. "Jeffrey? Kitty?"

"Come on," Jared said. As he steered Simon away from the wreckage of their room, he caught sight of the hall closet. The shelves were dripping with lotions and shampoos, which had also soaked the scattered towels. And at the bottom, near deep scratches in the wallboard, the secret door to Arthur's library had been ripped off its hinges.

"How did they find it?" Mallory asked.

Simon shook his head. "I guess they ransacked the place looking for it."

Jared crouched down and wriggled into

Arthur Spiderwick's library. Bright sunlight streaming through the single window showed the damage clearly. Tears burned his eyes as he stepped across a carpet of shredded pages. Arthur's books had been ripped free of their bindings and scattered. Torn sketches and toppled bookshelves littered the floor. Jared looked around the room helplessly.

"Well?" Mallory called.

"Destroyed," Jared said. "Everything's destroyed."

"Come on," Simon called. "We have to get that goblin."

Jared nodded his head, despite the fact that neither his brother nor his sister could see him, and moved numbly toward the door. There was something about the desecration of this one room—a room that had remained secret all these years—that made Jared feel as

"Everything's destroyed."

though nothing would ever be right again.

Together he, Simon, and Mallory trudged up the stairs to the attic, crossing over glittering pieces of smashed holiday ornaments and stepping past a broken dress form. In the dim light Jared could see dust erupting in time with the clattering of griffin claws, and he could hear more screeching above them.

"One more level and we can step right onto the roof," Jared said, pointing to the final staircase. It led to the single highest room in the house, a small tower with half-boarded windows on all four sides.

"I think I heard some barking," Simon said as they climbed. "That goblin must still be okay."

When they reached the top of the tower, Mallory swung her sword at the window boards, splintering them. Jared tried to pry off what was left loose.

"I'll go first," Simon said, hopping onto the ledge and gingerly climbing past the jagged slats and onto the roof.

"Wait!" Jared shouted. "What makes you think you can control that griffin?" But Simon didn't seem to be paying attention.

Mallory strapped on a belt, wrapping it around the sword so it hung from her hip. "Come on!"

Jared swung his legs over the sill and stepped out onto the slate. The sudden sunlight almost blinded him, and for a moment his blurry eyes scanned the forest beyond their lawn.

Then he saw Simon approaching the griffin, who had cornered the goblin against one of the brick chimneys. The goblin was Hogsqueal.

"Stop gawping, snail-heads!"

Chapter Two

IN WHICH an Old Friend Returns

"Stop gawping, snail-heads!" Hogsqueal yelled. "Help me!" He was backed against a chimney, one hand holding his coat closed over a largish object, the other brandishing an empty slingshot menacingly.

"Hogsqueal?" Jared grinned at the sight of the hobgoblin, then stopped with a scowl. "What are you doing here?"

Simon was holding the griffin back, mostly by standing between him and Hogsqueal and yelling loudly. Byron turned his hawk head to the side and blinked, then pawed the ground with his talons as though he were more feline than bird. Jared suspected that Byron thought they were playing a new game.

Hogsqueal hesitated, seeing Jared's face. "I didn't know this was *your* house until the griffin showed up."

"You helped catch our mother?" Jared could feel his face growing warm. "Trash our house? Kill Simon's pets?" He took two steps toward Hogsqueal, hands fisting. He'd *trusted* Hogsqueal. He'd *liked* him. And the hobgoblin had *betrayed* them. Jared could barely think with the roaring in his ears.

"I didn't kill anything." Hogsqueal opened his coat a little, revealing a marmalade ball of fur.

"Kitty!" Simon said, distracted by the sight of the kitten.

In that moment Byron lunged past Simon,

catching the hobgoblin's arm in his beak.

"Aaaaaaahhhhh!" Hogsqueal screamed. The cat yowled, jumping onto the roof.

"Byron, no!" Simon yelled. "Drop him!"

The griffin shook his head, whipping Hogsqueal back and forth. The hobgoblin's shouts became louder.

"Do something!" Jared called, panicked.

Simon stepped up to the griffin and hit him hard on the beak with his hand. "NO!" he shouted.

"Oh crap, don't do *that*!" Mallory said, reaching for the sword at her waist. But instead of attacking, the griffin stopped shaking Hogsqueal and looked at Simon with something like alarm.

"Drop him!" Simon repeated, pointing to the slate roof.

Hogsqueal struggled ineffectually, pushing

"I'm sorry, gobstoppers."

his fingers into Byron's nose slits and trying to bite the feathery neck with his baby teeth. The griffin ignored the hobgoblin but didn't make a move to put him down either.

"Be careful," Jared told his brother. "Better he eats Hogsqueal than us."

"Noooo! I'm sorry, gobstoppers," Hogsqueal said, still writhing. "I didn't mean it! Honest. Get me out of here! Heeeeeelp!"

"Jared," Simon said. "Grab Hogsqueal, okay?"

Jared nodded, edging nearer. This close, he could smell the griffin—it had a feral scent, like a cat's fur.

Simon put one hand on the top of Byron's beak, the other on the bottom, and started to lever them apart, repeating, "Be a gooooood boy. Yes. Drop the goblin."

"*Hob*goblin!" Hogsqueal yelped.

"Are you crazy?" Mallory hollered at her brother. The griffin turned his head abruptly in her direction, almost knocking Simon sprawling.

"Sorry," Mallory said in a much smaller voice.

Jared gripped Hogsqueal around the legs. "Got him."

"Hey, yaffner, we're not going to be playing tug-of-war with my body, right? Right?"

Jared just smiled grimly.

Simon tried again to push Byron's beak open. "Mallory, come and help me. Grab the bottom of the beak, and I'll get the top."

She stepped carefully across the slanted roof. The griffin eyed her nervously.

"When I say pull," Simon said, *"pull."*

Together they tried to pry the griffin's jaws apart. Mallory's fingers slid into Byron's mouth as she strained, nearly hanging from the griffin, trying to use her weight against him. Byron struggled and then suddenly gave in, opening his mouth and dropping Hogsqueal's full weight into Jared's arms. Losing his balance, Jared slid backward on the shingles, letting go of Hogsqueal and scrabbling for a handhold. The hobgoblin slid as well, knocking loose the shingle Jared was gripping on to. Jared slipped and grabbed hold of the gutter moments before he would have fallen off the side of the house.

Simon and Mallory looked at Jared with wide eyes. He swallowed hard. As they moved to haul him back onto the roof, Jared saw Hogsqueal make for the open window.

"He's getting away!" Jared said, trying to pull himself higher. His elbow dug into the dried leaves and mud that clotted the gutter.

"Forget about the stupid goblin," Mallory said. "Grab hold of me."

They hauled him back onto the roof. As soon as he was upright, Jared ran after Hogsqueal with Mallory and Simon close behind. They thundered down the stairs.

Hogsqueal was sprawled in the hall outside their bedrooms, and yellow yarn was wrapping itself around him. Jared gaped as the yarn tied itself in a bow.

Thimbletack hopped up on Hogsqueal's head. "I will help you fight the fey. I believe I've a debt to pay."

Jared looked at the yarn and then back at Thimbletack. "I didn't know you could do that!" He remembered how his shoelaces had seemed to tie themselves together and suddenly had an explanation.

The little brownie grinned. "Being unseen

"He's getting away!"

is not enough to get things clean."

"Hey," Hogsqueal yelled. "Get this crazy kipper off me! I wasn't running out on you. I was escaping from that tooby monster on the roof!"

"Shut up," Mallory said.

"That goblin is not misunderstood," said Thimbletack. "He is just plain no good."

"That noddy brownie's a fine one to talk," said Hogsqueal.

"You're going to tell us everything you know, or we're going to spread ketchup on you and put you right back up on the roof," said Jared. Right then he was so angry that he meant every word of it.

Thimbletack jumped down onto the leg of an overturned coffee table. "That would be overly kind to a goblin in a bind. No, we'll set rats to nibble off your toes, poke out your eyes, and put them up your nose. Your fingers we'll remove with dull scissors, and we'll wait until your confidence withers."

Simon paled but said nothing.

Hogsqueal squirmed in his bindings. "I'll tell you already, surly-boots. No need to threaten!"

"Where is our mom?" Jared demanded. "Where would they have taken her?"

"Mulgarath's lair is at the dump on the edge of town. He's built a palace of trash, and it's defended by his goblin army and by other things besides. Don't be a pumpkin-head.

There is no way you can get in there."

"What other things are defending it?" Jared demanded.

"Dragons," Hogsqueal said. "Little ones, mostly."

"Dragons?" Jared repeated in horror. Arthur's field guide had notes on dragons, but Arthur himself had never seen one. All of his accounts were secondhand. But even second-hand, the stories were frightening—they described poisonous venom, teeth as sharp as daggers, and bodies that were as quick as whips.

"And you were part of Mulgarath's goblin army?" Mallory asked, eyes narrowed.

"I had to be!" Hogsqueal exclaimed. "Everyone was joining up! Where was I sup-posed to go, chatter-basket?"

"What did you tell them happened to the

other goblins—the ones you were with before?"

"*Other* goblins?" Hogsqueal said. "For the last time, lily-pants, I'm a *hob*goblin! You might as well call a blackbird a crow!"

Jared sighed. "So, what *did* you say?"

Hogsqueal rolled his eyes. "What do you think, beetle-guts? I said a troll ate 'em, simple as that."

"If we untie you, will you take us to the dump?" Mallory demanded.

"Probably too late." Hogsqueal grunted.

"What was that?" Jared scowled.

"Yes," Hogsqueal said. "*Yes!* I'll take you. Are you happy, snotters? Just as long as I don't have to see that griffin again."

"But, Jared," Simon said, a small smile twisting his mouth, "it would be a lot faster if we flew."

"Wait, now! I didn't agree to that!" Hogsqueal exclaimed.

"We need a plan," Mallory said, stepping away from the hobgoblin and lowering her voice. "How can we beat an army of goblins, a dragon, and a shape-shifting ogre?"

"There has to be something," said Jared, following her. "They must have a weakness." The pages of Arthur's Guide that had once been so clear in his mind had faded, his memory growing increasingly spotty. He tried to concentrate, to remember anything that might be important.

"Too bad we don't have the field guide." Simon stared at the broken fish tanks as though some answer could be found among the glass shards.

"But we know where Arthur is," said Jared carefully, a plan starting to form in his mind. "We could ask him."

"Just how are you suggesting we do that?" Mallory asked, one hand on her hip.

"I'm going to ask the elves to let me talk to him." Jared spoke as though that were a perfectly reasonable suggestion.

Mallory's eyes widened with surprise. "The last time we saw the elves, they weren't exactly what I would call *friendly*."

"Yeah, they wanted to trap me underground forever," said Simon.

"You have to trust me," Jared said slowly. "I can do it. They promised that they wouldn't hold me there against my will ever again."

"I trust *you*," said Mallory. "It's the elves I don't trust, and you shouldn't either. I'm going to come."

Jared shook his head. "There isn't enough time. Get Hogsqueal to tell you everything he knows about Mulgarath. I'll be back as soon as I can." He looked down at the little brownie. "I'll bring Thimbletack—if he'll come."

"I thought it had to be just you," said Simon.

"I have to be the only human," Jared said, his eyes still fixed on Thimbletack.

"I have not been out of the house in years." With that, Thimbletack walked to the edge of the chair and let Jared put him into the hood of Jared's sweatshirt. "But I must put aside my fears."

They left before Simon or Mallory could talk them out of it. Crossing the street, they started up the hill toward the elven grove. The late-morning sky had deepened to a bright, cloudless blue, and Jared hurried, afraid that they didn't have much time.

"It is true I took the book."

Chapter Three

IN WHICH Jared Finds Out Things
He Doesn't Want to Know

The grove was the same as he remembered it—tree-rimmed with mushrooms
in the center—but this time when Jared
stepped into the middle, nothing happened. No
branches laced together to trap him, no roots
wound around his ankles, and no elves
appeared to scold him.

"Hello!" Jared yelled. He waited a moment,
but the only reply was the distant calling of
birds.

Frustrated, Jared paced back and forth. "Is

anyone here? I'm kind of in a hurry!"

Still nothing. Minutes passed.

Looking at the ring of mushrooms, he had an overwhelming urge to strike out at the elves. If only they hadn't taken Arthur.

He'd just lifted his foot to kick one when he heard a soft voice from the tree line.

"Reckless child, what are you doing in this place?" It was the green-eyed female elf, her hair tinged with more reds and browns than it had been before. And her gown was now deep amber and gold, like summer giving way to fall. Her voice sounded more sad than angry.

34

"Please," Jared said. "Mulgarath has my mother. I have to save her. You have to let me talk to Arthur."

"What should I care for one mortal?" She turned toward the trees. "Do you know how many of my own people have been lost? How many dwarves—old as the stones beneath our feet—are no more?"

"I saw it," Jared said. "We were there. Please—I'll give you anything. I'll stay here if you want."

She shook her head. "The only thing you had that was of value to us is lost."

Jared felt relief and terror at the same time. He needed to see Arthur, but he had nothing else to offer. "We didn't have the Guide," he said. "We couldn't have given it to you then, but maybe we can get it back now."

The green-eyed elf turned back with a

scowl. "I have no further interest in your tales."

"I . . . I can prove it." Jared reached back into his hood, pulled out Thimbletack, and set him down in the grass. "I told you our house brownie had the book. This is Thimbletack."

The little brownie took off his hat and made a low bow, trembling slightly. "Great Lady, I know how this must look, but it is true I took the book."

"Your manners become you." She glanced at them both and then was silent for a moment.

Jared shifted impatiently as Thimbletack climbed up Jared's leg and slid back into his hiding place. The green-eyed elf's silence unnerved Jared, but he forced himself to stay quiet. This might be their last chance to convince her.

Finally she continued. "Our time to punish and to command is past. The moment we feared is upon us. Mulgarath has gathered a great army and is using the Guide to make it even more fearsome."

Jared nodded, although he was puzzled. He couldn't think of anything Mulgarath could do with the Guide that would make an army more dangerous. It was just a book.

"Promise me this, mortal child," the green-eyed elf said. "If Arthur's field guide comes again into your possession while you look for your mother, you will give it to us so that it can be destroyed."

Jared nodded, giddily agreeing to anything that meant he would be able to see Arthur. "I will. I'll bring it—"

"No," she said. "When it is time, we will come to you." She pointed upward and spoke something in a strange language. A single leaf spiraled from a high branch of an old oak. It drifted slowly, as though it were falling through water instead of air. "Your audience with Arthur Spiderwick will last as long as it takes that leaf to fall to the ground."

Jared looked up toward where she pointed. As slowly as the leaf was moving, it still seemed too fast. "What if that isn't enough time?"

She smiled coldly. "Time is something that neither of us has the luxury of anymore, Jared Grace." But Jared barely noticed, because walking toward them from the trees was a man in a tweed coat, with graying patches of hair on the sides of his balding head. Leaves swept around him and dropped in a carpet in front of him so that his feet never touched the ground. He adjusted his spectacles nervously and peered at Jared.

Jared could not help grinning. Arthur Spiderwick looked just like the picture in the library. Now everything would be all right. His great-great-uncle would explain what to do, and that would be that.

"Uncle Arthur," Jared began. "I'm Jared."

A man in a tweed coat

"I do not believe I could possibly be your uncle, child," Arthur said stiffly. "To the best of my knowledge, my sister has no sons whatsoever."

"Well, actually, you're my great-great-uncle," Jared said, suddenly unsure of himself. "But that's not important."

"That's nonsense."

This wasn't going the way it was supposed to at all. "You've been gone a long time," Jared explained carefully.

Arthur scowled. "A few months, perhaps."

Thimbletack spoke up, climbing out of his hiding place and onto Jared's shoulder. "Listen to the boy—it is the only way. We cannot afford to delay."

Arthur peered down at the brownie and blinked twice. "Hello, old man! How I have missed you! Is my Lucy well? What about my wife? Will you give them a message for me?"

"Listen!" Jared interrupted. "Mulgarath has my mother, and you're the only one who knows what to do."

"Me?" Arthur asked. "Why should I know what to do?" He pushed his spectacles higher. "I would imagine that I would advise —wait, how old are you?"

"Nine," Jared replied, dreading what would come next.

"I would say that you should stay safe and leave the handling of such dangerous creatures to your elders."

"Didn't you hear me?" Jared shouted. "MULGARATH HAS MY MOTHER. THERE ARE NO ELDERS!"

"I understand," Arthur said. "However, you must —"

"No, you *don't* understand!" Jared couldn't

stop himself. It felt too good to finally just scream at someone. "You don't even know how long you've been here! Lucinda is older than you now! You don't know *anything*."

Arthur opened his mouth as if to speak and then closed it. He looked pale and shaky, but Jared found it hard to care. His eyes burned with unshed tears. On the other side of the ring of mushrooms the single leaf was drifting ever closer to the ground.

"Mulgarath is a very dangerous ogre," Arthur said quietly. He didn't look at Jared when he spoke. "Even the elves do not know how to stop him."

"He has a dragon, too," Jared said.

Arthur looked up suddenly with interest. "A dragon? Really?" Then he shook his head and his shoulders slumped. "I can't tell you how to deal with any of this. I'm sorry—I simply don't know."

Jared wanted to plead, to demand, but no words came.

Arthur took a step closer, and when he

spoke, his voice was very gentle. "Child, if I always knew what to do, would I be here, trapped with the elves, never to see my own family again?"

"I guess not," Jared said, closing his eyes. The leaf had reached his height. It wouldn't be long now before his time was up.

"I can't give you a solution," Arthur said. "All I can give you is information. I wish I could do more."

He continued. "Goblins run in small packs, usually no more than ten. They follow Mulgarath because they're afraid of him—otherwise you would never see so many in one place. Without him leading them, they would fall into squabbling. But even with him, they probably aren't very organized.

"As for ogres, Mulgarath is typical of their kind. They're master shape-shifters—clever, sly,

A. SPIDERWICK

and cruel. Strong, too, unfortunately. One flaw that might help you is that they are often vain and prone to bragging."

"Like in the 'Puss in Boots' story?" Jared asked.

"Exactly." Arthur's eyes gleamed as he spoke. "Ogres think a lot of themselves and want you to think a lot of them as well. They love to hear themselves talk. And the normal protections—like that garment you're wearing— are next to useless. They're too powerful.

"As for dragons . . . well, I must confess everything I know about them was culled from other researchers."

"Other researchers? You mean there are other people researching faeries?"

Arthur nodded. "All over the world. Did you know there are faeries on every continent? There are variations, of course, much like with any other animal. But I digress.

"The subtype of dragon is probably of the European wyrm variety most common to this region. Very poisonous. I remember one account where a dragon lived on cow's milk — it got huge and its venom poisoned everything, scorched the grass, and made the water undrinkable."

"Wait!" Jared exclaimed. "Our water burns your mouth if you drink it — our well water."

"A very bad sign." Arthur sighed heavily and shook his head. "Dragons are quick, but they can be killed the same as any other creature. The difficulty, of course, is the poison. It

"A very bad sign."

grows stronger as the dragon grows, and only a very small number of creatures are fast enough and brave enough to go after a dragon, the way a mongoose attacks a cobra."

Jared looked at the leaf—it was almost to the ground. Arthur followed the look. "My time talking to you is almost done. Will you give Lucinda a message for me?"

"Sure. Of course." Jared nodded.

"Tell her—" But whatever Arthur was going to say was lost in the leaves that whorled around him, obscuring him from view. A tornado of leaves circled upward and then . . . nothing. Jared looked for the elf, but she was gone as well.

As Jared left the boundary of the grove, he saw Byron clawing in the dirt. Simon sat on the griffin's back, petting the creature to calm it. Behind him, Mallory held the dwarven sword

"It's your turn to trust us."

aloft, the metal gleaming in the sun. Hogsqueal sat at the beast's neck, looking positively miserable.

"What are you doing here?" Jared asked. "I thought you said you trusted me."

"And we do," said Mallory. "That's why we waited here instead of rushing in and hauling you out."

"We even have a plan." Simon held up a loop of rope. "Come on. You can tell us what you found out from the elves on the way."

"So, now," said Mallory, "it's your turn to trust us."

"I caught the humans."

Chapter Four

IN WHICH Everything Goes into the Fire

As he crossed the highway, Jared tried not to jostle the deliberately loose knots that kept his hands bound behind his back. He marched behind a similarly bound Mallory and avoided looking up at the distant shadow of Byron and Simon flying overhead—their only means of escape if things were to go wrong and the quickest way out if things were to go right.

Hogsqueal poked Jared with the tip of the dwarven sword. "Hurry up, nose pickers."

"Cut it out," Jared said, nearly stumbling.

Thimbletack squirmed against the back of his neck. "We're not even inside yet, and that thing is sharp," Jared said.

"Right," the hobgoblin snickered. "My bad, lump-meat."

"Leave Jared alone, or I'm going to *show* you how to use a sword," Mallory hissed, then suddenly went still.

The trees on that side of the highway were almost entirely leafless, blackened, and dead. The few remaining leaves hung from the branches like bats. The trees looked less real than the dwarves' ironwood trees. Just beyond, Jared could see the junkyard.

The gate was rusted open, and the worn dirt path was overgrown with patches of dead weeds. A NO TRESPASSING sign was stuck in the ground at an odd angle. Old cars, tires, and other trash were stacked in haphazard piles that resembled swells of sand along a beach. And ahead Jared could see the palace clearly. Its spires gleamed with glass and tin in the full light of the sun.

Jared saw several goblins peering out of the rusted heap of a car. Two sniffed the air and a third began to bark. Then the goblins started to crawl from the vehicle. Each lifted a toadlike head and gnashed teeth of glass and bone. They carried dwarf-forged pikes and curved swords.

"You say you captured both?"

"Say something," Jared whispered to Hogsqueal.

"I caught the humans," Hogsqueal called. "No thanks to you trash hounds!"

A large goblin scuttled closer. His teeth were made of bottle glass, and they shimmered in the sunlight—brown, green, and clear. He was dressed in a ragged coat with tarnished buttons and a frayed tricornered hat. The hat in particular caught Jared's eye because it was dyed a strange ruddy brown. Flies buzzed close. "You say *you* captured both?"

"Easily, O large Wormrat," Hogsqueal bragged. "There they were, the girl swinging around this sword right here—sharp, isn't it?—but I was too fast for them! I . . ." Wormrat eyed him, and the hobgoblin's words trailed off. "Okay," he started again. "They were sleeping and I—"

The goblins began to bark loudly. Whether it was laughter or something else, Jared wasn't sure.

"I still caught the scallywags! They're *my* prisoners," Hogsqueal said, raising Mallory's sword. It looked huge in his small hands and was wobbling slightly.

Wormrat barked, and the tip of the sword drooped. Jared glanced upward to see if Simon and Byron were nearby, but they were either well hidden or gone. Jared hoped for what seemed like the millionth time that Simon would be able to control the griffin.

"We do what *I* say," said Wormrat. "Bring them!"

Mallory and Jared were pushed and pulled through the junkyard by a barking mass of goblins. They had to be careful not to step on the jagged pieces of metal that stuck up from the dry dirt at odd angles. Whenever Mallory and Jared slowed, the goblins shoved them and poked them with weapons. Rust from the cars streaked Jared's jeans as he squeezed through the narrow passageways between them. Finally they were led into a clearing where a dozen more goblins were lazing around a fire. Smallish bones were scattered among the debris.

Wormrat grunted and pointed toward a blue car close to the fire. "Tie the prisoners there."

"We should take them to the Palace of Trash," Hogsqueal said, but he sounded halfhearted.

"Quiet!" barked the big goblin. "*I* give commands."

A grinning goblin used a coil of rusty wire to attach Jared and Mallory's tether to the car. As the goblin wrapped the cord around the side mirror, Jared could smell his rotten breath and could see his strange, mottled skin, the hair tufting from his ears, the dead white of his eyes, and the long, quivering whiskers that stuck up from his face. The other goblins stood in a circle, leering and waiting.

"Back to your posts, lazy dogs!" bellowed the large goblin. Then, turning to the goblins that had already been there when he arrived, he scowled. "And the prisoners had better be where I leave them! I go report them to Mulgarath!" Barking, most of his goblins trickled back to their patrols as he left, but a few remained behind to sit around the fire.

Jared wriggled his hands. He was sure the knots were still loose enough for him to get free, but he was less sure they were going to be able to get past all of those goblins.

Jared and Mallory sat in the cold, sandy dirt for what felt like hours, watching the goblins pick up small lizards and toss them into the fire. The sky began to darken, the sun lighting slashes of gold across the waning day.

"Maybe this wasn't such a great plan after all," Mallory said softly. "We're nowhere near Mom, and I don't know where Simon is."

"But we're almost there," Jared whispered back. Their hands were close enough that he could take one of hers and squeeze it.

"What are they waiting for?" she asked with a groan.

"Maybe for the big one to come back," Jared replied.

Across the fire one of the goblins threw a wriggling black thing into the flames. "They never burn," the goblin said. "I wish they would burn."

"You still couldn't eat 'em," said another.

A soft voice from Jared's hood reminded him that Thimbletack was still with them. "Take a gander," whispered the brownie, "salamander."

Jared looked near his legs. One of the lizardlike things was next to his shoe. It was an opalescent black, with front legs and a long body that tapered to a tail. It was swallowing what appeared to be the tail of another.

"Jared," Mallory said. "Look in the fire. What are they?"

He leaned forward as far as his bonds would let him. There in the flames were all of the salamanders he'd seen the goblins toss. But instead of being scorched, they were sitting calmly as the blaze burned around them. As Jared stared, a few of the creatures moved slightly, one twisting its head and another scuttling deeper into the blaze. They really were immune to the fire.

He tried to think back to Arthur's Guide. He thought there was something on salamanders, but the images blurred in his mind. These little creatures looked like another illustration, but he couldn't quite put his finger on it. He was too nervous to concentrate—too full of thoughts of his mother and brother and of the goblins so close by.

A few moments later one of the goblins scurried over and poked Jared's stomach with a dirty claw. "They look so tasty. I could bite off one whole rosy cheek. I bet it would be sweet as candy." A long line of drool hit the dirt next to Jared.

Jared swallowed and looked over at Hogsqueal. The hobgoblin was using the dwarven sword to poke at the fire. He didn't look up, and that made Jared even more nervous.

Another goblin followed Jared's glance. "Wormrat will think he did it," the goblin said, pointing to Hogsqueal. "He was making a fuss before."

Hogsqueal stood up. "Of all the monkey-toasted, cracker-jack-headed . . ."

A third goblin approached, running its tongue over jagged teeth. "So much meat."

"Get away from him!" Mallory said. She pulled her hand out of Jared's. Only then did Jared realize he'd been clutching Mallory so tightly that his fingernails had dug into her skin.

"Would you rather we ate *you* instead?" asked the goblin sweetly. "Sugar and spice and everything nice. If that's what little girls are made of . . . sounds tasty to me!"

"Eat this!" Mallory said. She pulled her hands free and punched him in the face.

"The sword!" Jared yelled to Hogsqueal, trying to work his wrists out of the rope. The hobgoblin glanced at Jared once, then dropped the dwarven sword and ran from the clearing.

"Coward!" Jared yelled furiously. Free of his bindings, he ran toward the fire, but two goblins grabbed hold of his legs and toppled him into the dirt. Crawling forward until his hand could reach the blade, Jared swung the sword hilt-first to his sister. His hand stung, and he realized with dazed fascination that he had cut himself. More goblins jumped onto his back, pinning him in the dirt.

"Get away from him!" Mallory advanced, sword flashing as she swung it through the air. The goblins backed away from her. She whipped the blade at them. The goblins leaped off Jared and scrambled for their own weapons.

"Go! Run!" she yelled. A goblin jumped on her back, biting her shoulder.

Jared grabbed the goblin's arm and tugged it off his sister. Mallory kicked another that

"Get away from him!"

was approaching. One of the goblins picked up a dwarf-forged pike and swung it at Mallory. She parried it and then lunged, stabbing the goblin with her blade. As the creature howled, Mallory froze, realizing what she'd done. Blood stained the silver sword. The goblin fell, but others were rushing up fast and Mallory was still staring.

A screech above them broke her trance. Byron swooped toward the clearing and the goblins scattered, diving underneath trash for cover. The griffin's wings beat heavily, making the dirt dance.

"Come on," Jared said, grabbing at Mallory's arm. Together they leaped onto the rusted hood of a station wagon and then jumped down into a narrow path of corroded fencing. They ran past an overturned bathtub and a stack of tires. A series of doors were leaned up against a refrigerator, and as they passed them, Jared stopped abruptly. There, lying on a carpet of corrugated metal, was a cow.

It was a massive structure.

Chapter Five

IN WHICH They Find the Meaning of "Here There Be Dragons"

By reflex, Jared looked behind him, but the goblins were no longer there. The riffin landed with a clatter of claws on top of car, denting it, and immediately began to room himself like a cat. Simon grinned from Byron's back.

Jared turned to Mallory, but she was staring at the cow. It was chained to the ground, owing softly, eyes wide enough to show the whites. Her udder was covered in what ppeared to be writhing black snakes jostling

for a position at her reddened teats. They
blackened the metal sheeting on the ground
beneath her like a squirming carpet. After a
moment Jared realized the creatures were
larger salamanders.

"What are those things doing?" Mallory
asked. The bloodstained sword hung limply
from her hand, and Jared was overwhelmed
with the impulse to take it from her and clean
it before she'd have a chance to notice.

He stepped closer to the cow instead. "Drinking the milk, I think."

"Ugh," Simon said, squinting down from Byron's back. "Weird."

Several more salamanders were lying in the dirt, their scales dull and their bodies wriggling. They were far larger than the tiny finger-length ones Jared and Mallory had seen in the fire.

"They're shedding their skin," Simon said. "What *are* they?"

Jared shook his head. "Fire-resistant salamanders. But they aren't supposed to get big like this. They look almost like . . ." But he wasn't quite sure what it was they reminded him of. Something nagged at the back of his mind.

At that moment Byron darted forward and seized one of the wriggling black creatures in his beak, tossed it into the air, and gulped it down. Then he seized another and another.

Greedily he went for an even larger one, as long as Jared's arm, curled up in the sun. It turned and hissed, and suddenly Jared knew what he was looking at.

"They're dragons," he said. "They're all dragons."

Out of the corner of his eye Jared saw something moving toward them, fast as a whip. He whirled, but the black thing hit him hard in the chest. Falling backward, he only had time to throw his hands up over his face before the thick body of a dragon as long as a couch scrabbled over him. Jared's head struck the ground, and for a moment everything went hazy.

"Jared!" Mallory howled. The dragon opened its mouth to show hundreds of teeth,

thin as needles. Jared froze. He was too terrified to move. His skin burned where the slick
body had touched him.

Mallory chopped hard with her sword,
catching the dragon's tail. Black blood spurted
as the dragon turned toward her.

Jared got to his feet, dizzy and shivering.
His skin was reddened, and the cut he'd gotten
earlier throbbed angrily. "Watch out," he
called. "It's poisonous!"

"Byron!" Simon yelled, pointing
toward the black shape
that was hurtling
after Mallory.
"Byron!
Get it!"

The griffin swung up into the air with a screech. Jared looked after Byron and Simon desperately. How would Mallory escape the dragon now? She was cutting and thrusting as best as she could, but the dragon was too fast. Its body coiled and leaped like a snake, small forearms clutching and gripping, mouth so wide it seemed like it could swallow her whole. Mallory couldn't last. Jared had to do something.

Jared grabbed the nearest thing—a piece of metal—and hurled it at the dragon. The creature spun again and started toward him, lightning fast, jaws open. It hissed.

The griffin streaked down from the sky, talons reaching for the dragon, beak ripping at its back. The dragon coiled around Byron, wrapping its tail tight enough to choke. Simon hung on desperately as the griffin's wings

The dragon coiled around Byron.

THE DRAGON

pushed them back up
into the air. The dragon
twisted, teeth sinking
into Byron's feathered
and furred body. Then
the griffin's wings
missed a beat, and in
the sudden drop
Simon slipped off.

Jared ran toward his
twin as he plummeted
toward the junkyard. Simon
fell onto a pile of screen windows
and his left arm twisted at an odd angle.

"Simon?" Jared knelt down beside him.

Simon moaned softly and used his other arm
to push himself into a sitting position. His left
cheek and neck were red from dragon poison,
but the rest of his skin looked far too pale.

"Are you okay?" Jared whispered. Mallory touched Simon's arm gingerly.

Simon winced and stood up shakily. Above them the dragon and griffin were locked together, a writhing, looping knot of scales and skin. The dragon's teeth were embedded deep in Byron's neck, and the griffin was flying erratically.

"He's going to die." Simon limped toward the cow with her mass of dragon fingerlings.

"What are you doing?" Jared called after him.

When Simon turned back to them, tears were running down his face. As Jared watched him, Simon—who had never killed anything, who always carried spiders outside—stepped on the head of one of the baby dragons, crushing it into a smear under his shoe. It squealed. Dragon blood stained the ground and melted the edge of Simon's heel.

"Look!" he screamed. "Look what I'm doing to your babies!

The dragon turned in midair, and Byron seized the opportunity. Plunging his beak into the creature's neck, he rent it wide. The dragon went limp in Byron's claws.

"Simon! You did it!" Mallory said.

Simon watched Byron land near them. His feathers were smeared with blood, and he shook himself. Then, dropping the body of the large dragon, Byron resumed eating the babies.

"This isn't going the way we planned," Simon said.

"But we're closer to the palace now," Jared said. "Mom has to be there."

"Do you think you can make it, Simon?" Mallory asked, although she didn't look very well herself, with her cheek cut and her jacket slashed at the shoulder.

Simon nodded, his face grim. "I can, but I don't know about Byron."

"We have to leave him here," Jared said. "I

think he'll be okay. The poison doesn't seem to affect him."

Byron gulped down another squirming black salamander and regarded the Grace kids with his strange golden eyes. Simon petted him carefully on the nose. "Yeah, he seems to like these dragons more than anything I used to feed him."

"Let me see if I can do something about your arm," Mallory said. "I think it's broken." She used her undershirt to tie Simon's arm neatly against his side.

"Are you sure you know what you're doing?" Simon asked, wincing.

"Sure I'm sure," Mallory said, tying the white fabric tight.

They marched in the direction of the palace. It was a massive structure made of what looked like cement or stucco, mixed with gravel, glass, and aluminum cans. It looked less molded than poured and in some places resembled dried lava. The windows were strangely shaped, as though the creator had fitted the house around whatever refuse he had found. Lights flickered inside. Several spires came to delicate points off the main roof, which was black with tar and covered in overlapping layers of glass and tin that looked like fish scales. As Jared got closer, he noticed that the main gate was made of old brass headboards. Beyond the gate was a deep trench dug in the earth, studded with jagged, rusty metal and chunks of broken glass. The drawbridge was down.

"Shouldn't there be goblins guarding it or something?" Mallory asked.

The drawbridge was down.

Jared looked around. In the distance he could see tendrils of smoke coming from what he guessed were goblin camps.

"It's going to be dark soon," Simon said.

"It just seems too easy," Jared said. "Like a trap."

"Trap or not, we're going to have to keep going," Mallory said.

Simon nodded. Jared still thought that Simon looked a little too pale and wondered how much pain he was in. At least the red skin had faded somewhat.

Stepping onto the drawbridge cautiously, Jared braced himself for something to happen. He kept glancing at the jagged glass jutting up out of the moat. Then he raced across. Mallory and Simon paused a moment, then ran after him.

As they entered the palace, they found

themselves in a large hall constructed from salvaged materials and what seemed to be cement. The archways were trimmed with bent chrome fenders. Hubcaps hung from the ceiling on rusted chains, flickering with the uncertain light of dozens of yellowed candles and dripping with wax. Set inside one wall was a fireplace large enough to roast Jared in.

It was eerily quiet. Their footsteps echoed in the dim rooms, and their shadows loomed along the walls.

They walked farther, passing musty-smelling couches covered in threadbare throws.

"Do we have anything even remotely resembling a plan?" Mallory asked.

"Nope," Jared said.

"No," Simon echoed.

"Hush," said Thimbletack. "Have a care. I hear something over there."

They paused a moment, listening. There was a faint noise that sounded almost like music.

"I think it's coming from here," Jared said, pushing open a door that had been decorated with more than a dozen knobs. Inside the room was a tall, long table made from a plank of wood on top of three sawhorses. Thick candles that smelled of burning hair covered most of the table. Rivulets of melted wax ran down the sides. Also set on the table were platters of food—long, greasy trays of roasted frogs, half-eaten apples, the tail and bones of a large fish. Flies buzzed greedily around the remains. From somewhere in the room came a series of high-pitched notes.

"What is that?" Simon asked, squeezing past a single large chair. Then he stopped, looking at something Jared and Mallory couldn't see. They scrambled over to him.

A large urn sat on the floor underneath an open window. There, in the wavering light, Jared could see sprites trapped in honey, sinking as though it were quicksand. The sprites' tiny cries were the sound he had heard before.

Simon reached in to pull the sprites free, but the honey was heavy and clung to their thin wings, tearing them. The sprites squealed as he set each one down on the table in a sticky, sodden heap. One was completely still and lay there limply, like a doll. Jared looked away, staring out the window.

"Do you think there are more in there?" Mallory whispered.

"I think so," Simon said. "At the bottom."

"We have to keep going." Jared moved toward another doorway. The thought of the tiny drowned faeries made him feel queasy.

"The palace is just too quiet," said Mallory as she followed him.

"Mulgarath can't be here all the time," Jared said. "Maybe we got lucky. Maybe we can just find Mom and get out."

Mallory nodded, but she didn't look convinced.

They passed by a map hung on a wall. It looked much like Arthur's old map, but the places had been renamed. Jared noticed that over the junkyard had been written MULGARATH'S PALACE and that lettered across the entire top of the paper was MULGARATH'S DOMAIN.

"Look!" Simon said. Ahead of them was a large room with a throne at its center. Surrounding the throne were overlapping carpets in different patterns, all of them moth-eaten and worn. The throne was made of metal, welded together and jagged in places.

At one end of the room was a spiral staircase, each step a plank suspended on two long metal chains. The whole thing looked like a web, wobbling slightly with each breeze. In the dim light the stairs looked impossible to climb.

Mallory pulled herself onto the first rung. It swung alarmingly. She tried to step onto the next one, but her legs were too short.

"These steps are too far apart!" she exclaimed.

"Perfect for an ogre," Simon pointed out.

She finally managed to catch the second step, flop onto it chest-first, and pull herself up that way.

The stairs looked impossible to climb.

"Simon's not going to be able to climb this," she said.

"I can . . . I'll be okay," Simon insisted, lifting himself awkwardly onto the first step.

Mallory shook her head. "You're going to fall."

"Hold on tight," Thimbletack called from Jared's hood. "You'll be all right." Then Jared watched in amazement as each step swung closer and held steady for his siblings to climb onto it. With one working arm and Mallory's help, Simon climbed up the stairs.

"It would behoove you to move," said Thimbletack.

"Oh, right." Jared worked his way up the steps. Even with the brownie's help, his heart thundered as he went higher and higher. The cut on his hand burned where he gripped the chains. Glancing down into the darkness below made Jared momentarily dizzy.

At the top they found themselves in a hall-way with three doors, all mismatched.

"Let's try the middle one," Simon said.

"We made so much noise just now," said Mallory. "Where is everyone? It's eerie."

"We have to keep going," Jared said, repeating his words from earlier.

Mallory sighed and opened the door. It opened onto a large room with a balcony made of mismatched stones and chains. Giant cathedral windows, filled with translucent mosaics made of glass shards, covered the other wall. Their mother was in one corner, bound, gagged, and unconscious. In the other corner, hanging from ropes and a pulley, was their dad.

"What are you doing here?"

Chapter Six

IN WHICH All Hell Breaks Loose

"W"hat are you doing here?" Jared asked. Behind him he heard Simon and Mallory exclaim "Dad!" together. Their father's black hair looked slightly mussed and his shirt was untucked on one side, but it was definitely him.

Their father's eyes went wide. "Jared! Simon! Mallory! Thank goodness you're okay."

Jared furrowed his brow. Something about this didn't feel right. He looked around the

95

room again. Out beyond the balcony he saw goblins milling in the gloom, holding torches. What was going on?

"Quick," Mallory said. "We have to move. Jared, untie Mom. I'll work on Dad."

Jared leaned down and touched his mother's pale cheek. It felt cold and clammy. Her glasses were gone. "Mom's unconscious," he said.

"Is she breathing?" Mallory asked, halting.

Jared put his hand against his mother's lips and felt the ghost of her breath. "She's okay. She's alive."

"Did you see Mulgarath?" Simon asked his father. "The ogre?"

"There was some commotion outside," Mr. Grace said. "I didn't see anything after that."

Mallory fumbled with the pulley and managed to lower her dad's hands. "How did they get you all the way from California?"

Their dad shook his head wearily. "Your mother called to say how worried she was—all three of you acting strange and then going missing. I came as soon as I could, but the monsters were already at the house. It was terrible. At first I couldn't believe what was happening. And they kept talking about a book. What is this book?"

"Our uncle Arthur—" Jared began.

"More like Mom's great-uncle, our great-great-uncle," Mallory said as she picked at the knots.

"Right. Well, he was interested in faeries." Jared untied his mother as he talked, but even free from her bonds, she didn't move. Jared smoothed back her hair, wishing she would open her eyes.

"His brother got eaten by a troll," Simon put in.

RICHARD GRACE

Jared nodded, looking nervously around. How long before they were discovered? Did they really have time for this? Now that they had found their mother, they had to get out as quickly as possible. "And so he made this book that was all about faeries. It had stuff in it that even some of the faeries themselves didn't know."

"Because they mostly don't bother with one another, it seems," Mallory said.

How were they going to get their mother down the stairs? Could their dad carry her? Jared tried to concentrate on explaining. They had to make sure their dad would understand. "But the faeries didn't want one guy to have that much power over them, so they tried to get the book back. When he wouldn't give it to them, they took him instead."

"The elves did," Simon said.

"Really?" said their father with a strange gleam in his eye.

Jared sighed. "Look, I know it sounds unbelievable, Dad, but look around. Does this look like the set of one of your movies?"

"I believe you," their father said softly.

"To make a very long story short," Mallory said, "we found the book."

"Except we lost the book again," said Simon. "The ogre has it."

"And he's got a really idiotic plan to take over the world," Mallory put in.

Their father's eyebrows rose, but he only

said, "So, now that the book is gone, all of the knowledge is gone with it. There's no other copy? That seems like a shame."

"Jared remembers a lot," Simon said. "I bet he could make a book of his own."

Mallory nodded. "And we learned some stuff along the way—right, Jared?"

Jared smiled, looking down. "I guess so," he said finally. "But I wish I remembered more."

Their father flexed his newly freed wrists and stretched his legs. "I'm sorry that I wasn't here sooner. I shouldn't have left you kids and your mom alone. And I want to make it up to you. I want to stay."

"We missed you too, Dad," Simon said.

Mallory looked down at her boots. "Yeah."

Jared said nothing. Something about this was too easy. It just felt wrong. "Mom?" he said softly, and shook her.

Dad spread his arms wide. "Come and give your father a hug."

Simon and Mallory embraced him. Jared looked down at his mother and reluctantly started to cross the room, when his dad said, "I want us all to be together from now on."

Jared froze. He wanted it so much to be true, but it didn't feel true. "Dad would never say that," he said.

His father grabbed hold of his arm. "Don't you *want* us to be a family again?"

"Of course I do!" Jared yelled, jerking his arm free and stepping back. "I want Dad to be less of a jerk, and for Mom to not be sad. I want my dad to stop talking about himself and his movies and his life all the time and remember that I'm the loser who almost got kicked out of school and Simon is the one who likes animals and Mallory is the fencer. But that's not going to happen and *you're not him.*"

As Jared looked up into the familiar hazel eyes of his father, they started to turn pale yellow. His father's body elongated, filling out, becoming a mammoth shape clad in the tattered remains of ancient finery. His hands became claws, and his dark hair twined together into branches. "Mulgarath," Jared said.

The ogre wrapped one arm around Mallory's neck and with the other arm grabbed Simon.

"Come here, Jared Grace!" Mulgarath's voice boomed, far deeper than their father's. He strode toward the balcony, still holding Simon and Mallory. "Give yourself up. Otherwise, I will heave your brother and sister into my moat of glass and iron."

"Leave them alone," Jared said shakily. "You have the book."

"You're not him".

"I can't do that," Mulgarath said. "You know the secret that speeds the growth of dragons and how to kill them. You know the weaknesses of my goblins. I cannot allow you to make another Guide."

"Run!" Mallory yelled. "Get Mom and run!" She bit the ogre.

He laughed and pressed his arm tighter against her, heaving her up into the air. "Do you think your feeble strength is enough to match mine, human girl?"

Simon kicked, but the hulking monster didn't seem to notice.

A groan came from the other end of the room, and Jared half turned. His mother stirred and opened her eyes. They went wide. "Richard? I thought I heard . . . oh my God!"

"Everything's going to be okay, Mom," Jared said, wishing for his voice to stay even. Somehow her seeing all of this made it more horrible.

"Mom, tell him to run!" Mallory shouted. "Both of you! Go!"

"Quiet, girl, or I'll break your neck." The ogre growled, but when he addressed Jared, his voice became soothing. "It's a fair trade, isn't it? Your life for the lives of your brother and sister and mother?"

"Jared, what's happening?" their mother called.

Jared tried to stay calm. He was afraid to die, but it would be so much worse to watch his brother, sister, and mother get hurt. Already the ogre's fingers seemed to be loosening, ready to drop Simon and Mallory at any moment. "You won't free us—even if I promise not to make another Guide!"

Mulgarath shook his head slowly, eyes full of dark satisfaction.

"Put them down!" Their mother's voice was panicked. "Put my children down! Jared, what are you doing?"

It was then that Jared noticed Mallory's sword lying on the floor.

Seeing the sword made Jared focus. He had to concentrate—to come up with a plan. Jared remembered what Arthur had said about ogres—they liked to brag. He only hoped that this one would. "I'll give up and come over there."

"No, you idiot!" Mallory shouted.

"Jared, don't!" Simon yelled.

"But before I do . . ." Jared swallowed hard and hoped that the ogre would take the bait. "There's something I want to know. Why are you doing all of this? Why now?"

Mulgarath smiled toothily. "You humans take everything and keep the best part for

"Why are you doing all of this?"

yourselves. You live in palaces, dine on banquets, and clothe yourselves in fine silks and velvets like royalty. We, who live forever, who have magic, who have *power*, are supposed to lie down and let your kind trample us into the ground. No more.

"I have been planning this for a long time. First I thought I would have to wait for my dragons to mature. I have time on my side. But with the Guide I was able to step up my plans. As long as they have enough milk, the dragons are quite docile, you know. And I am sure by now you've realized how fast the milk makes them grow and how powerful they become.

"The elves are too feeble to stop me, and the humans will never see it coming. It is my time—the time of Mulgarath! The time of goblins! The land will have a new master!"

Jared tipped his head to the side, hoping Mulgarath was too busy talking to notice, and whispered into his hood. "Thimbletack, can you make the chains on the railing attach to Mallory's and Simon's legs?"

Thimbletack wriggled and whispered back. "I'd have to get to the ground without making a sound."

"I'll keep him talking," Jared whispered, then raised his voice, addressing the ogre. "So why did you have to kill the dwarves? I don't understand. They wanted to help you."

"They had their own little dream of a world built of iron and gold. But what fun would it be to rule a world like that? No, I want a world of flesh and blood and bone." The ogre smiled again, as though pleased with the way that had sounded, then looked down at Jared. "Enough talk. Come here."

"What about the Guide?" Jared asked. "A
least tell me where that is."

"I think not," Mulgarath said. "It is beyond
you now."

"I just want to know if I could have found
it," Jared said.

A cruel smile twisted the ogre's features.
"Indeed, had you been more clever, you could
have found it. A pity that you are a mere
human child, no match for me at all. The book
was beneath my throne this whole time."

"You know," Jared said, "we killed your
dragons. I hope that doesn't put too much of a
dent in your clever plan."

Mulgarath looked genuinely surprised
Then his brow knotted with anger.

Out of the corner of his eye Jared could see
the chains unlinking and snaking across the
floor like vipers. One wrapped around

Mallory's leg, and the other circled Simon's waist. When the metal touched her skin, Mallory flinched. A third chain crept toward Mulgarath's ankle, and Jared hoped that the ogre would not notice.

But Jared's pause was enough to catch Mulgarath's attention. He looked down and spotted Thimbletack skittering along the floor. The ogre kicked the brownie, his giant foot tossing Thimbletack across the room, where Thimbletack landed like a crumpled glove beside Mrs. Grace. The chains stopped moving. "What is this?" Mulgarath bellowed, stamping down on the links near his foot. "You sought to trick me?"

Jared ran forward and grabbed Mallory's silver sword.

Mulgarath laughed and dropped Simon and Mallory off the side of the balcony. They both screamed and then were silent, while their mother's scream went on and on. Jared didn't know if the chains had held. He didn't know anything.

Jared thought he might be sick. Rage filled him. Everything looked small and far away. He felt the weight of the sword in his hand as though it were the only real thing in the world. He raised it high. Someone far away was calling his name, but he didn't care. Nothing mattered anymore.

Then just as he was about to swing, he saw the look of satisfaction on the ogre's face—as if Jared were doing just what Mulgarath had expected . . . as if Jared were playing right into his hands. If he swung the sword, he would be matching his strength against the ogre's, and the ogre would win.

Abruptly Jared changed the direction of his blow and brought the point of the sword down hard, stabbing Mulgarath in the foot.

The ogre howled with surprise and pain, lifting his wounded foot. Jared dropped the sword and grabbed the chain that ran beneath the ogre's other foot, pulling with his full weight. Mulgarath stumbled backward, trying to regain his balance. But just as his calves hit the chain fence, Jared slammed into him again. The ogre's weight pulled the chains loose from the wall, and he went hurtling over the side.

Jared rushed to the edge of the balcony. To his immense relief, Simon and Mallory were dangling over the pit, chains wrapped around Simon's waist and Mallory's leg. They called up to him weakly.

Jared started to smile, but as he did, he saw Mulgarath, his fist clutching another chain, his body shifting into the shape of a squirming dragon. He began to writhe his way back up to them.

"Watch out!" Jared shouted.

Simon, hanging closer to the monster, tried to kick at it. He only made the chains swing dangerously.

Mallory and Simon screamed as Jared leaned out as far as he could and swung the sword again. This time it hit the ogre's chain, cutting through it and biting into the wall of the palace. Mulgarath started to transform once more. As the ogre fell toward the pit of jagged glass, his body became smaller and smaller until he finally became a swallow. The bird veered out of the pit, heading toward the assembled throng of goblins. In mere moments Mulgarath would lead that army into the palace. There would be no escape for the Grace family.

But then, as the bird turned, angling to fly back toward where the children stood, a hob-goblin's hand suddenly shot out and grabbed the bird out of the air. It happened so fast that Jared didn't have time to be surprised and the ogre didn't have time to shift again.

Hogsqueal bit off the bird's head and chewed twice with apparent enjoyment. "Cruddy mouth-breather," he said as he gulped it down.

Jared couldn't help it. He started to laugh.

"All this time and I never knew."

Epilogue

IN WHICH the Story of the Grace Children Comes to Its Conclusion

Jared sat down on the gleaming floor of Arthur's newly cleaned library and leaned against Aunt Lucinda's leg. Mallory knelt next to him, making stacks of old letters written in languages that none of them spoke. Simon flipped through an old book of sepia photographs while their mother poured hot tea into mugs.

All of that might have seemed normal if Hogsqueal wasn't seated on a nearby footstool, playing checkers with a bandaged and annoyed-looking Thimbletack.

Lucinda held up one of the paintings of the little girl from Arthur's desk. "I can't believe it. All this time and I never knew."

It had been three weeks since they had defeated Mulgarath, and Jared was finally starting to think things were going to *stay* okay. The goblins had dispersed into bickering groups. Byron was gone by the time they had left the palace, and he appeared to have eaten every last dragonet. Jared, Simon, Mallory, and their mother had all walked home from the dump. It had been a long walk, and they had been so tired that once they'd arrived home, they had collapsed into the piles of feathers and cloth that had been their beds without complaint or comment. It was dark when Jared had finally woken and noticed Thimbletack curled up on a pillow beside him, with Simon's tiny, marmalade cat nestled against the little brownie. Jared had smiled, taken a deep breath, and choked on the feathers.

Downstairs he'd found his mother cleaning up the kitchen. When Jared had walked into the room, she had hugged him tightly.

"I'm so sorry," she'd said.

Even though it had kind of made him feel like a baby, he'd hugged her back for a long time.

Later that week their mother had arranged for Lucinda to leave the asylum and come stay with them. Jared had been amazed to find his great-aunt, with a haircut and a new suit, sitting in the parlor one day after school. When Mulgarath died, his magic must have died with him, and although Lucinda often walked with a cane now, her back was as straight as it had ever been.

Mrs. Grace had been less miraculous in curing Jared's school troubles; he had been expelled. His mother had enrolled him and Simon in a private school nearby. She claimed the school had excellent art and science programs. Mallory decided to stay at the old school. She only had one year till she was in high school anyway and plenty still to prove to the J. Waterhouse fencing team.

For his part, Jared had locked Arthur's field guide in its metal trunk again. But after all that he still didn't know what to think. Were there creatures still after them? Had the ogre been the worst—or just the worst yet?

A breeze blew through the office, scattering papers and snapping Jared out of his thoughts. Simon jumped up, trying to catch hold of the letters.

"Did you leave a window open?" their mother asked Aunt Lucinda.

"I don't recall doing so," their great-aunt replied.

"I'll get it," Mallory said, and started toward the window.

Then a single leaf blew inside. It danced in the air, swooping and swirling, until it fell directly in front of Jared. The leaf was greenish brown, and Jared thought it might be from a maple tree. Written on the leaf in a delicate hand was Jared's name. He turned it over and read:

The time has come
Meet us tonight
under the full moon
Bring the book

"It doesn't say where," Mallory said, reading over his shoulder.

"The grove, I guess," Jared said.

"You're not going to go, are you?" Simon asked.

"I'm going," said Jared. "I promised. I need to give them Arthur's field guide. I don't want anything like this to happen again."

"Then we're going with you," said Simon.

"I'm coming too," their mother said.

The three children looked at her with surprise, then glanced at each other.

"Don't forget me, dizzinits," Hogsqueal said.

"Don't forget *us*," Thimbletack corrected.

Aunt Lucy reached for her cane. "I hope it isn't much of a walk?"

That night they left the house carrying lanterns, flashlights, and the field guide. It was weird to go looking for faeries with their mother in tow and Simon helping Aunt Lucy along. Up the hill they went, and then they carefully made their way down the other side.

Jared thought he heard a whisper of "Clever is as clever does," but it might have been only his memory or the wind.

The grove was lit with dozens upon dozens of sprites, whirring through the air, twinkling like giant fireflies, alighting on tree branches and settling in the grass. Elves sat on the ground—many more than the three the children had seen on their first visit—all clad in the deep colors of autumn as though to camouflage themselves with the forest.

The elves went quiet as the small group of humans made their way to the center of the clearing. There, standing among all of those seated, was the green-eyed elf, her expression unreadable. Beside her stood the leaf-horned elf, looking stern, and red-haired Lorengorm, who was smiling.

Thinking of Thimbletack, Jared made an awkward bow. The others followed his example.

"We brought the book," Jared said, and held it out to the green-eyed elf.

She smiled. "That is well. We must abide by our promises, and had you not, Simon would have had to stay with us for a very long time."

Simon shivered and stepped closer to Mallory. Jared scowled.

"But since you have done so," she continued, "we wish to return it to you for safekeeping."

"What?" Mallory said. Jared was astonished.

"You have proven that humans may use the

knowledge it contains for good. Therefore we return the Guide to you."

Lorengorm stepped forward. "We also wish to give you some measure of our gratitude for restoring peace to these lands. To that end we offer you a boon."

"A boon?" Hogsqueal puffed out his chest. "What do I get? How come these ninnyhammers get a reward when I'm the one that defeated Mulgarath?"

Several of the elves began to laugh, and Thimbletack gave Hogsqueal a stern look.

"Figures he wasn't coming along to be supportive," Mallory said.

"So what would you like, little hobgoblin?" asked the green-eyed elf.

"Well," Hogsqueal said, putting a finger to his mouth as if considering. "I'd like some kind of medal, definitely. Gold, with 'fearsome killer of ogres' on it. No, wait, how about 'supreme slayer of monsters'? Or—"

"Is that all?" asked Lorengorm.

"It should say 'supreme beetlehead,'" Simon whispered to Jared.

"I don't think so," said the hobgoblin. "I want a victory feast in my honor. And it should have quail's eggs—I love those—and pigeon baked in a pie shell and barbequed ca—"

"We'll consider your requests," the green-eyed elf said, barely hiding a smile behind her delicate hand. "But now I must ask the children to name the desire of their heart."

Jared looked at his brother and sister. At first they seemed thoughtful, and then smiles started to grow on their faces. Jared glanced back at his mother, who still seemed a bit confused, and his great-aunt, her face full of hope.

"We would like our great-great-uncle, Arthur Spiderwick, to have a choice whether to stay in Faerie or not."

"You understand," Lorengorm said, "that if he chooses to return to the mortal world, the first time his foot touches the earth, he will become dust and ash."

Jared nodded. "I understand."

"We have anticipated your request," said the green-eyed elf. With a wave of her hand the trees parted, and Byron stepped through. On his back was Arthur Spiderwick.

Jared heard the others gasp behind him. Arthur smiled at Jared briefly, and this time Jared noticed that his eyes were like Lucinda's, both sharp and kind. Arthur sat on the griffin awkwardly and petted him with a kind of awe. Then he looked over at Mallory and Simon. He adjusted his glasses.

"You are my great-great-niece and nephew, aren't you?" he said softly. "Jared didn't mention that he had a brother and a sister."

Jared nodded. He wondered if there was any way he could apologize for the things he

"This is fine work."

had said earlier. He wondered what Arthur thought of him.

"I'm Simon," said Simon. "This is Mallory, and this is our mom." Simon looked at Lucinda and hesitated.

"I'm glad to meet you," said Arthur. "You three children clearly have my inquisitive blood running through your veins. You might have had cause to regret it." He shook his head wryly. "It seems to have gotten you into a lot of scrapes. Luckily you three seem far more adept at getting yourselves out of trouble than I ever was." He smiled again, and this time his smile wasn't the least bit tentative. It was a wide grin that made him look very unlike the man in the painting.

"We're glad to see you too," Jared said. "We want to give your book back to you."

"My field guide!" Arthur said. He took it from Jared's hands and started flipping through it. "Look at this—who did these sketches?"

"I did," Jared said, his voice as soft as a whisper. "I know they aren't very good."

"Nonsense!" Arthur said. "This is fine work. I predict that you are going to be a great artist someday."

"Really?" Jared said.

Arthur nodded. "Really."

Thimbletack walked up to Arthur's shoes. "Good to see you, my old friend, but there are some things to mend. Here is Lucinda, who you know. She is not as she was long ago."

Arthur's breath caught as he finally recognized her. *She must look so old to him,* Jared thought. He tried to picture his mother as a young woman, looking at an elderly version of him, but it was too hard, too sad.

Lucinda smiled, and tears ran down her

cheeks. "Daddy!" she said. "You look just the way you did the day you left."

Arthur made a move to dismount.

"No!" Lucinda said. "You'll turn to dust." Leaning on her cane, she walked closer to where he stood.

"I'm sorry for all of the sadness I caused you and your mother," he said. "I'm sorry I tried to trick the elves. I should have never taken the risk. I've always loved you, Lucy. I always wanted to come home."

"You are home now," said Lucinda.

Arthur shook his head. "Elven magic has kept me alive too long. I have lived past the span of my years. It is my time to go, but seeing you, Lucy—I can go without sorrow."

"I just got you back," she said. "You can't die now."

Arthur bent down and spoke to her—soft

words that Jared could not hear—before he stepped off the griffin and into her embrace. As Arthur's foot touched the ground, his body turned to dust and then smoke. It swirled around Jared's great-aunt and then whirled up into the night sky and was gone.

Jared turned to Lucinda, expecting to see her crying, but her eyes were dry. She stared up at the stars and smiled. Jared slid his hand into hers.

"It's time for us to go home," Aunt Lucinda said. Jared nodded. He thought about every thing that had happened, all of the things that he had seen, and suddenly realized how much he still had to sketch. After all, he was only at the beginning.

Here ends the tale of

THE GRACE
CHILDREN

About TONY DiTERLIZZI . . .

A *New York Times* bestselling author, Tony DiTerlizzi created the Zena Sutherland Award–winning *Ted*, *Jimmy Zangwow's Out-of-This-World Moon Pie Adventure*, as well as illustrations in Tony Johnston's Alien and Possum beginning-reader series. Most recently, his brilliantly cinematic version of Mary Howitt's classic *The Spider and the Fly* was awarded a Caldecott Honor. In addition, Tony's art has graced the work of such well-known fantasy names as J.R.R. Tolkien, Anne McCaffrey, Peter S. Beagle, and Greg Bear as well as Wizards of the Coast's *Magic The Gathering*. He and his wife, Angela, reside with their pug, Goblin, in Amherst, Massachusetts. Visit Tony on the World Wide Web at www.diterlizzi.com.

and HOLLY BLACK

An avid collector of rare folklore volumes, Holly Black spent her early years in a decaying Victorian mansion where her mother fed her a steady diet of ghost stories and books about faeries. Accordingly, her first novel, *Tithe: A Modern Faerie Tale,* is a gothic and artful glimpse at the world of Faerie. Published in the fall of 2002, it received two starred reviews and a Best Book for Young Adults citation from the American Library Association. She lives in West Long Branch, New Jersey, with her husband, Theo, and a remarkable menagerie. Visit Holly on the World Wide Web at www.blackholly.com.

Tony and Holly continue to work day and night fending off angry faeries and goblins in order to bring the Grace children's story to you.

Through field, cave, and forest
this yarn has unspun
with our heroes victorious
and evil undone!

Yet all is not merry
as we reach this end
and must bid farewell
to a father, guide, . . . friend.

Though Arthur is taken
what's given is vast!
His beloved Lucinda
is safe home at last.

Hogsqueal has eaten.
The Graces can rest.
And Thimbletack's back to
what brownies do best.

With everyone happy
and no longer vexed,
one question needs answering. . . .
What happens next?

Are there more ogres
and dragons to slay?
Is there more mayhem,
perhaps, on the way?

TONY DITERLIZZI

Ask Tony and Holly.
They'll swear that it's true.
But you still won't believe
what's coming for you!

For the time is upon us.
The Guide is at hand.
Soon Spiderwick's opus
will be read through the land.

HOLLY BLACK

So keep your eyes open.
And when you see it, do choose it!
Because knowledge is good. . . .
Just beware how you use it.

ACKNOWLEDGMENTS

Tony and Holly would like to thank
Steve and Dianna for their insight,
Starr for her honesty,
Myles and Liza for sharing the journey,
Ellen and Julie for helping make this our reality,
Kevin for his tireless enthusiasm and faith in us,
and especially Angela and Theo—
there are not enough superlatives
to describe your patience
in enduring endless nights
of Spiderwick discussion.

The text type for this book is set in Cochin.
The display types are set in Nevins Hand and Rackham.
The illustrations are rendered in pen and ink.
Art director: Dan Potash

For my darling Lucy
— love Papa

Watercolor study of Arthur and Lucinda Spiderwick, found in Arthur's study.

Me and Kaminski

Me AND Kaminski

Daniel Kehlmann

Translated from the
German by
Carol Brown Janeway

PANTHEON BOOKS, NEW YORK

Library of Congress Cataloging-in-Publication Data

Kehlmann, Daniel, [date]
[Ich und Kaminski. English]
Me and Kaminski / Daniel Kehlmann ; translated from
the German by Carol Brown Janeway.
p. cm.
ISBN 978-0-307-37744-9
I. Janeway, Carol Brown.   II. Title.
PT2671.E32I3413 2008
833'.914—dc22
2008003920

www.pantheonbooks.com
Printed in the United States of America
First American Edition
2   4   6   8   9   7   5   3   1

What a singular being do I find myself! Let this my journal show what variety my mind is capable of. But am I not well received everywhere? Am I not particularly taken notice of by men of the most distinguished genius? And why? I have neither profound knowledge, strong judgment, nor constant gaiety. But I have a noble soul which still shines forth, a certain degree of knowledge, a multiplicity of ideas of all kinds, an original humor and turn of expression, and, I really believe, a remarkable knowledge of human nature.

—James Boswell, *Journals*, December 29, 1764

Me and Kaminski

I

I AWOKE as the conductor knocked on the door of the compartment. It was a little after 6 a.m., we'd be there in half an hour, had I heard him? Yes, I muttered, yes, and dragged myself up into a sitting position. I had been lying across three seats, alone in the compartment, my back hurt and I had a stiff neck. My dreams had been shot through with the persistent racket that comes with any journey, voices in the corridor, announcements about platforms; they were unpleasant dreams, and I was jolted out of them repeatedly; once someone had yanked open the compartment door from outside in the corridor and coughed, and I had to get up to shut it. I rubbed my eyes and looked out the window: raining. I put on my shoes, took my old shaving kit out of my suitcase, yawned, and went outside.

The mirror in the toilet showed me a pale face, a mess of hair, and a cheek still imprinted with the pattern of the seat upholstery. I plugged in the shaver, nothing happened. I opened the door, saw the conductor still down at the other end of the car, and called out that I needed help.

He came and gave me a look and a thin smile. The shaver, I said, wasn't working, clearly there was no current. Of course there's current, he replied. No, I said. Yes, he said. No! He shrugged, perhaps it's the wiring, but in any case there's nothing he can do. But surely, I said, it's the very least one can expect from a conductor. He wasn't a conductor, he said, he was a train escort. I said I really didn't care. He asked me what I meant. I said I really didn't care what the job was called, it was superfluous anyway. He said he wasn't going to let himself be insulted by me, I should watch out, he might just bust me in the chops. He could try, I said, I was going to file a complaint in any case, and I wanted his name. He wasn't going to do any such thing, he said, and what's more, I stank and I was getting a bald spot. Then he turned around and went away cursing.

I shut the door to the toilet and took a worried look in the mirror. Of course there was no bald spot; where on earth did that ape get an idea like that? I washed my face, went back to the compartment, and

put on my jacket. Outside the window railroad tracks, electricity poles, and wires began to form a tightening grid, the train was slowing down, and the platform was already in sight: billboards, telephone booths, people with luggage carts. The train braked and came to a halt.

I pushed my way along the corridor toward the door. A man jostled me, and I pushed him aside. The conductor was standing on the platform. I handed down my suitcase. He took it, looked at me, smiled, and let it fall smack onto the asphalt. "Sorry," he said, and grinned. I climbed down, picked up the suitcase, and walked away.

I asked a man in uniform about my connecting train. He gave me a long look, then fished out a crumpled little book, tapped his forefinger thoughtfully against his tongue, and began to thumb the pages.

"Don't you have a computer?"

He gave me a questioning look.

"Doesn't matter," I said. "Keep going."

He thumbed, sighed, thumbed again. "Intercity 6:35. Track 8. Then change . . ."

I moved on quickly, I had no time for his chatter. Walking wasn't easy, I wasn't used to being awake at such an early hour. My train was standing at track 8. I boarded it, entered the carriage, pushed a fat lady

aside, worked my way to the last free window seat, and let myself fall into it. A few minutes later we were on our way.

Straight opposite me was a bony man wearing a tie. I nodded to him, he returned the greeting and then turned his eyes away. I opened my suitcase, took out my notepad, and laid it on the narrow table between us. I almost knocked his book off, but he was able to grab onto it in time. I had no time to lose, my article was already three days overdue.

Hans Bahring, I wrote, *who has made many* . . . no! . . . *numerous attempts to bore us to death* . . . yes, that's it . . . *with his insights*, no, *badly researched insights into lives of important*, no, *prominent*, no, that's even worse. I thought for a moment . . . *historical personalities, has come up with another one. To call his just-published biography of the artist*, no, *painter Georges Braque a failure would probably be to overpraise a book that* . . . I stuck the pencil between my teeth. Now I needed something really to the point. I pictured Bahring's face when he read the article, but that didn't give me any ideas either. This was less fun than I'd thought it would be.

I was probably just tired. I rubbed my chin, the stubble felt unpleasant, I simply had to get a shave. I put down the pencil and leaned my head against the windowpane. It was starting to rain. Drops were hitting the glass and streaming in the opposite direc-

tion from the one we were traveling in. I blinked, the rain got heavier, the raindrops seemed to make little exploded puddles full of faces, eyes, and mouths. I closed my eyes, and while I listened to the drumming of the water, I dozed off: for a few moments, I didn't know where I was; I felt I was floating through the huge emptiness of space. I opened my eyes: the glass was covered with a film of water, and trees were bowed under the force of the rain. I closed my notepad and put it away. Then I noticed the book the man in front of me was reading: *Picasso's Last Years* by Hans Bahring. I didn't like this. I had the feeling I was being mocked somehow.

"Lousy weather," I said.

He looked up for a moment.

"Not very good, is it?" I pointed to Bahring's hash-up.

"I find it interesting," he said.

"That's because you're not an expert."

"That'll be why," he said, and turned the page.

I leaned my head against the neck rest, my back was still hurting from the night in the train. I took out my cigarettes. The rain was easing up, and the first mountains were becoming visible through the haze. I used my lips to pull a cigarette out of the pack. As I clicked the lighter, I flashed on Kaminski's *Still Life of Fire and Mirror*: a flickering dazzle of bright

colors out of which a lancelike flame came leaping, as if it were trying to shoot clear of the canvas. What year? I didn't know. I had to prepare better.

"This is a nonsmoking carriage."

"What?"

The man didn't look up, just pointed to the sign on the window.

"Just a couple of quick puffs!"

"This is a nonsmoking carriage," he said again.

I dropped the cigarette and ground it out with my foot, clenching my teeth with fury. Okay, if that's how he wanted it, I wouldn't talk to him. I pulled out Komenev's *Some Thoughts on Kaminski*, a badly printed paperback with an unattractive thicket of footnotes. It had stopped raining, blue sky could be seen through gashes in the clouds. I was still very tired, but I couldn't allow myself to go to sleep again, I was going to have to get off any time now.

Very shortly afterward, I was wandering shivering through the main hall of a station, a cigarette in my mouth and a paper cup of steaming coffee in my hand. In the toilet I switched on my shaver, it didn't work. God—no current here either. The bookstore had a revolving paperback holder outside: Bahring's *Rembrandt*, Bahring's *Picasso*, and of course the window display had a pile of hardcover copies of *Georges Braque, or the Discovery of the Cube*. In a drugstore I

bought two throwaway razors and a tube of shaving cream. The local train was almost empty, the upholstered seats were soft, I leaned into them and immediately closed my eyes.

When I woke again, there was a young woman sitting opposite me, with red hair, full lips, and long, narrow hands. I looked at her, she pretended not to notice. I waited. When her eyes crossed mine, I smiled. She looked out the window. But then she hastily smoothed back her hair, she was having trouble concealing her nervousness. I looked at her and smiled. After a minute or two, she stood up, took her purse, and left the carriage.

Silly creature, I thought. Most likely she was waiting for me in the dining car, but so what, I had no desire to get up and follow her. The heat was sticky now: the haze was making the mountains seem close for a moment, then distant again, the soaring cliffs were draped in shreds of clouds, villages flew by, churches, cemeteries, little factories, a motorcycle crawling along a path between the fields. Then more meadows, woods, meadows again, men in overalls smearing steaming tar on a road. The train stopped, I got out.

A single platform, an arched canopy outside, a little house with shutters, a stationmaster with a mustache. I asked about my train, he said some-

thing, but it was in dialect and I didn't understand. I asked again, he tried again, we looked helplessly at each other. Then he took me to the big wall display with all the departure times. Naturally I had just missed my train and the next one wasn't for another hour.

I was the only guest in the station restaurant. Up there? That's quite a long way, said the proprietress. Was I going to spend my vacation up there?

On the contrary, I said. I was on the way to Manuel Kaminski.

It wasn't the best time of year, she said, but I'd surely have a couple of good days at best. She could promise me.

To Manuel Kaminski, I said again. Manuel Kaminski!

Don't know him, she says, he's not from around here.

I said, he's been living here for twenty-five years.

Exactly, she said, not from around here, she knew she was right about that. The kitchen door flew open, a fat man set a plate of greasy soup in front of me. I looked at it uneasily, swallowed a little, and said to the proprietress how beautiful I thought it was to be here. She smiled proudly. Here in the countryside, in nature, even here in this station. Way away from everything, among simple people.

She said what did I mean.

Not among intellectuals, I explained, overeducated posturing types with university degrees. Among people who were close to their animals, their fields, and the mountains. Who went to sleep early and got up early. Who lived, instead of thinking!

She stared at me as she frowned, and went away; I counted out the money on the table. I shaved in the wonderfully clean toilet: I had never yet been good at it, the shaving-cream got mixed with blood, and when I'd washed it off, dark stripes were suddenly spreading across my red, naked-looking face. Bald spot? Where on earth did he get that idea? I shook my head and my mirror image did the same.

The train was tiny. Just two carriages behind a little engine, wooden seats, nowhere to put your suitcases. Two men in rough overalls, one old woman. She looked at me, said something incomprehensible, the men laughed, and we set off.

Straight up the mountain. The force of gravity pushed me against the wood, as the train leaned into a bend, my suitcase tipped over, one of the men laughed, I glared at him. Another bend. And another. I began to feel faint. A ravine yawned next to us: a vertiginous slope of grass sprouting the strangest thistles and way below them contorted evergreens. We went through a tunnel, the ravine opened to our

right, then another tunnel and it was back on our left. The air smelled of cow shit. A dull pressure made itself felt in my ears, I swallowed, and it disappeared, but a couple of minutes later it was back to stay. Now even the trees had run out, and there was nothing but fenced pastures and the outlines of mountains on the other side of the void. Another bend, the train braked, my suitcase fell over one last time.

I got out and lit up a cigarette. The dizzy feeling gradually subsided. Behind the station was the village street, and behind that a two-story house with a weathered wooden front door and open shutters: *Belview Boardinghouse, breakfast, good cooking.* A stag's head stared at me gloomily from one of the windows. No help for it, this was where I'd reserved, everything else was too expensive.

The reception desk was staffed by a large woman with her hair in an elaborate beehive. She spoke slowly, articulating every word, but I still had to concentrate in order to understand her. A shaggy dog was snuffling around on the floor. "Take the suitcase to my room," I said, "and I need an extra pillow, a coverlet, and paper. Lots of paper. How do I get to Kaminski's house?"

She set her sausage hands on the reception desk

and looked at me. The dog found something and ate it noisily.

"He's expecting me," I said. "I'm not a tourist. I'm his biographer."

She seemed to be thinking this over. The dog pushed his nose against my foot. I suppressed the urge to kick him.

"Behind here," she said, "up the path. Half an hour, the house with the tower. Hugo!"

It took me a moment to grasp that this was aimed at the dog. "Do people often ask for him?"

"Who?"

"I don't know. Vacationers. Admirers. Anyone?"

She shrugged her shoulders.

"Do you have any idea who this man is?"

She said nothing. Hugo grunted and let something drop out of his mouth; I made myself not look. A tractor chugged past the window. I thanked her for her help and went outside.

The path began behind the semicircle of the main square, went up in a double spiral above the rooftops, and then through some brownish field of rubble. I took a deep breath and set off.

It was worse than I'd expected. A few steps and my shirt was already sticking to my body. A warm mist was rising off the meadows, the sun was blazing,

sweat poured down my forehead. When I stopped to catch my breath, I had cleared the first two turns.

I took off my jacket and put it over my shoulders. It fell to the ground; I tried tying the sleeves around my hips. Sweat was getting into my eyes, I wiped it away. I made it up another two bends, then I had to rest.

I sat on the ground. A mosquito buzzed, high-pitched, then suddenly stopped somewhere close to my head; seconds later my cheek began to itch. The wet grass was beginning to soak my pants. I stood up.

The main thing was obviously to find the right rhythm between walking and breathing. But it didn't come to me, I kept having to stop, my whole body was soon wet, I was having to pant and my breath rattled, my hair was stuck to my face. Then there was a rumble, I leapt sideways in fright, a tractor overtook me. The man driving it looked at me with indifference, his head bobbing to the rhythm of the engine.

"Can I hitch a ride?" I yelled. He didn't pay any attention. I tried to keep pace with him and almost managed to jump on. But then I fell back and couldn't catch up with him, and watched as he climbed the hill away from me, grew smaller, then

disappeared around the next curve. His diesel smell hung in the air for quite some time.

Half an hour later, I was at the top, breathing heavily and hanging on to a wooden post. As I turned around, the slope seemed to plunge in one direction as the sky soared away in the other, and I clung to the post till the rush of vertigo eased. I was surrounded by sparse tufts of grass mixed with shale, and the path ahead of me fell away gently. I followed it slowly, and after ten minutes it ended in a small south-facing bowl of rock that held three houses, a parking place, and a black-topped road leading down to the valley.

Yes: a wide, tarred road! I had made a great big detour, not to mention the fact that I could have done the whole thing by taxi. I thought about the proprietress: this was going to cost her! The parking place held nine, I counted them, cars. The first name-plate said *Clure*, the second said *Dr. Glinzli*, the third said *Kaminski*. I looked at it for a while. I had to get myself used to the idea that he really lived here.

The house was large and graceless: two stories and a pointy decorative tower in an elephantine approximation of art nouveau. There was a gray BMW parked in front of the garden gate; it made me envious, I would love to have driven a car like that

just once. I smoothed back my hair, put on my jacket, and fingered the mosquito bite on my cheek. The sun was already low in the sky, my shadow on the lawn in front of me was narrow and long. I rang the bell.

II

APPROACHING FOOTSTEPS, a key turned, the door
flew open, and a woman in a dirty apron was giving
me the once-over. I said my name, she nodded, and
the door slammed.

Just as I was about to ring again, the door
reopened: another woman, mid-forties, tall and
thin, black hair, narrow, almost oriental eyes. I said
my name, she made a brief gesture that meant:
Come in. "We weren't expecting you until the day
after tomorrow."

"I was able to get here sooner." I followed her
through a bare hall, at the other end of which a door
stood open, emitting a babble of voices. "I hope it
won't cause you any problems." I gave her time to
confirm that it wouldn't indeed cause any, but she
didn't take me up on it. "You could have told me

17

about the road. I came up here on the path, I could have gone right over the edge. You're the daughter?"

"Miriam Kaminski," she said, quite coolly, and opened another door. "Please wait."

I went in. A sofa, two chairs, a radio on the windowsill. On the wall, an oil painting of a dark hilly landscape, probably Kaminski's middle period, early fifties. The wall above the heating unit was streaked with soot, in a couple of places dust hung down from the ceiling in threads that moved in some air current that was otherwise undetectable. I was going to sit down, but right then in came Miriam and, I recognized him at once, her father.

I hadn't expected him to be so small, so tiny and shapeless compared with the slim figure in old photographs. He was wearing a pullover and impenetrable dark glasses, one hand was on Miriam's arm and the other on a white walking cane. His skin was brown, creased like old leather, his cheeks sagged loosely, his hands seemed enormous, his hair a chaotic halo. He was wearing threadbare corduroys and gym shoes, the right one was undone and the laces dragged behind him. Miriam led him to a chair, he groped for the armrests and sat down. She remained standing and watched me.

"Your name is Zollner," he said.

I hesitated, it hadn't sounded like a question, and I was struck, quite inexplicably, by a momentary shyness. I held out my hand, met Miriam's stare, and pulled it back again; of course, stupid mistake! I cleared my throat. "Sebastian Zollner."

"And we're waiting for you."

Was that a question? "If it's okay with you," I said, "we can start right now. I've done all the preparation." Literally, I'd been traveling for the better part of two weeks. I had never spent so much time on a single project. "You'll be amazed how many old acquaintances I've found."

"Preparation," he repeated, "acquaintances."

I felt a stirring of unease. Did he understand what I was saying? His jaws were working, he laid his head to one side and seemed, but this was obviously a mistake, to be looking past me at the picture on the wall. I looked at Miriam for help.

"My father has very few old acquaintances."

"Few is misstating things," I said. "Let's just take Paris . . ."

"You must excuse me," said Kaminski. "I've just got out of bed. I spent two hours trying to get to sleep, then I took a sleeping pill, and then I got up. I need coffee."

"You're not allowed coffee," said Miriam.

"A sleeping pill before you get up?" I asked.

"I always wait till the very end, in case I can do it on my own. You're my biographer?"

"I'm a journalist," I said. "I write for several major newspapers. Right now I'm working on your life story. I've got a couple more questions, then as far as I'm concerned we can start tomorrow."

"Article?" He lifted one of his enormous hands and ran it over his face. His jaws worked. "Tomorrow?"

"You'll be working mostly with me," said Miriam. "He needs his peace and quiet."

"I don't need peace and quiet," he said.

Her other hand laid itself on his other shoulder. She smiled at me over his head. "The doctors see it differently."

"I'm grateful for any help," I said cautiously, "but naturally your father is the most important person to talk to. The source, quite simply."

"I'm the source, quite simply," he said.

I rubbed my cheeks. It wasn't going well. Peace and quiet? I needed my own peace and quiet, everyone needs peace and quiet! Ridiculous! "I'm a great fan of your father, his paintings have changed art . . . the way I see it."

"Rubbish," said Kaminski.

I began to sweat. Of course it was rubbish, but I'd

never yet met an artist who didn't believe this sentence. "I swear it!" I laid a hand on my heart, reminded myself that such a move would have zero effect on him, and quickly yanked it away again. "You have no greater admirer than Sebastian Zollner."

"Who?"

"Me."

"Oh, right." He lifted his head, then let it droop again, for a second I thought he'd really looked at me.

"We're glad you've taken over this project," said Miriam. "There were several applicants, but . . ."

"Not that many," said Kaminski.

". . . your publisher recommended you highly. He thinks a lot of you."

Hard to believe. I had met Knut Megelbach precisely once in his office. He had walked up and down, wringing his hands, when he wasn't using one hand to pull books out of the bookcase and stick them back again while the other was groping the coins in his pants pocket. I had been talking about the imminent Kaminski Renaissance: new dissertations were going to be written, the Pompidou Center was working on an exhibition, and there was also the sheer documentary value of his memories, one mustn't forget everything he'd seen and whom he'd known; Matisse had been his teacher, Picasso his

friend, Richard Rieming, great poet, his mentor. I was, I told him, well acquainted with Kaminski, a friend of his, actually, there was no doubt he would talk to me candidly. Only one small thing was lacking to ensure that everyone's interest would land on him, there would be articles in all the magazines, the price of his paintings would soar, and the biography would be a surefire success. "And what is that?" Megelbach asked. "You mean, what's missing? He needs to die, of course." Megelbach walked back and forth, thinking. Then he stood still and smiled at me.

"I'm glad," I said. "Knut's an old friend."

"What's your name again?" asked Kaminski.

"We need to get a couple of things straight," said Miriam. "We'd like . . ."

The sound of my cell phone interrupted her. I pulled it out of my pants pocket, saw who was calling, and switched it off.

"Who was that?" asked Kaminski.

"We would like you to show us everything you want to publish. In return for our cooperation. Agreed?"

I looked her in the eyes. I was waiting for her to look away, but oddly she didn't blink. After a few seconds I looked down at the floor and my dirty shoes. "Naturally."

"And as for old acquaintances, you will not use them. You have us."

"Got it," I said.

"Tomorrow I have to be away," she said, "but the day after tomorrow we can start. You will put your questions to me, and if necessary, I'll get further information from him."

For a few seconds I didn't say anything. I heard Kaminski's whistling breath, his lips smacked as they moved. Miriam looked at me.

"Agreed," I said.

Kaminski bent forward and had a coughing fit, his shoulders shook, he pressed a hand to his mouth, and his face went red. I had to restrain myself from giving him a thump on the shoulder. When it was over, he sat there stiffly, seemingly drained.

"Then everything's settled," said Miriam. "Are you staying in the village?"

"Yes," I said vaguely. "In the village." Did she want to invite me to spend the night in the house? Nice gesture.

"Good. And now we must get back to our guests. We'll see you the day after tomorrow."

"You have guests?"

"People from the neighborhood and our gallerist. Do you know him?"

"I spoke to him last week."

"We'll straighten that out," she said.

I had the feeling her mind was already on something else. Her grip as she shook my hand was surprisingly strong, then she helped her father onto his feet. The two of them moved slowly to the door.

"Zollner." Kaminski was standing still. "How old are you?"

"Thirty-one."

"Why are you doing this?"

"What?"

"Journalist. Several major newspapers. What do you want?"

"I find it interesting! You learn a lot and you can get involved in things that . . ."

He shook his head.

"I wouldn't want anything else!"

He banged his stick impatiently on the floor.

"I don't know, I—I fell into it somehow. Before, I was at an advertising agency."

"That explains it."

That had sounded odd; I looked at him, trying to understand what he'd meant. But his head was nodding down onto his chest and his expression was blank. Miriam led him out, and I heard their footsteps fade into the distance.

I sat down in the chair the old man had just been sitting in. Sunbeams were slanting in through the

window, and motes of dust were dancing in them. It must be nice to live here. I pictured it: Miriam was roughly fifteen years older than me, but I could live with that, she still looked good. He wasn't going to be around much longer, we'd have the house, his money, and there'd certainly be a few remaining paintings. I would live here, administer the estate, maybe set up a museum. I would finally have the time to write something really big, a fat book. Not too fat, but fat enough for the fiction shelves in the bookshops. If possible one of my father-in-law's paintings on the cover. Or maybe better to use something classical. Vermeer? Title in dark type. Stitched binding, heavy paper. Given my connections, I would get a couple of good reviews. I nodded, stood up, and went out.

The door at the end of the hall was now closed, but you could still hear the voices. I buttoned my jacket. It was time for decisiveness and being a man of the world. I cleared my throat and walked in fast.

A large room, table laid, and two Kaminskis on the walls: one pure abstract and the other a misty city view. People were standing around the table and at the window with glasses in their hands. As I came in, silence fell.

"Hello!" I said. "I'm Sebastian Zollner."

That broke the ice right away; I felt the mood

ease. I held out my hand to each of them in turn. There were two elderly gentlemen, one of them obviously a village dignitary and the other a banker from the capital. Kaminski muttered something to himself; Miriam looked at me thunderstruck and seemed to want to say something, but then stayed silent. A dignified English couple introduced themselves to me as Mr. and Mrs. Clure, the neighbors. "Are you the writer?" I asked. "I guess so," he said. And then of course there was Bogovic, the gallerist to whom I'd talked ten days before. He gave me his hand and looked at me thoughtfully.

"Are you still working?" I said to Clure. "Anything new?"

He threw a glance at his wife. "My new novel just came out. *The Forger's Fear.*"

"Brilliant," I said, giving him a slap on the upper arm. "Send it to me, I'll review it!" I smiled at Bogovic, who for some reason was behaving as though he didn't remember me, then I turned toward the table, where the housekeeper, with raised eyebrows, was laying another place. "Do I get a glass too?" Miriam said something quietly to Bogovic, he frowned, she shook her head.

We sat down at table. There was a totally tasteless soup made of apple and cucumbers. "Anna is an expert in my diet!" said Kaminski.

I began to tell them about my journey, the insolent conductor this morning, the clueless railroad employees, the incredibly changeable weather.

"Rain comes and goes," said Bogovic. "That's what it does."

"Keeps it in training," said Clure.

Then I told them about the proprietress at the boardinghouse, who really didn't know who Kaminski was. Could they imagine? I banged the table, glasses jingled, my mood was infectious. Bogovic slid his chair back and forth, the banker talked quietly to Miriam, I spoke louder, he fell quiet. Anna brought peas and cornbread, very dry, almost impossible to swallow, evidently the main course. There was a wretched white wine to go with it. I couldn't remember ever eating so badly.

"Robert," said Kaminski in English, "tell us about your novel."

"I wouldn't dare call it a novel, it's a modest thriller for unspoilt souls. A man happens to find out, by mere chance, that a woman who left him a long time ago . . ."

I began to tell them about my difficult climb. I imitated the man driving the tractor and the way he looked, and how the engine had made him shake from head to foot. My acting made everyone merry. I described my arrival, my shock when I discovered

the road, my investigation of the mailboxes. "Imagine! Glinzli! What a name!"

"What do you mean?" asked the banker.

"Listen, nobody can have a name like that!" I described Anna opening the door to me. At that very moment, she came in with the dessert; of course I jumped, but I knew instinctively that it would have been a major mistake just to stop talking. I imitated her gaping, and how she had slammed the door right in my face. I knew for sure that the person being imitated is always the last to recognize the imitation. And indeed, she set the tray down so hard that everything clattered, and left the room. Bogovic was staring out of the window, the banker had his eyes closed, Clure rubbed his face. Kaminski's lip-smacking seemed deafening in the silence.

Over dessert, a chocolate cream that was far too sweet, I told them about a piece I'd written on Wernicke, the artist who died so spectacularly. "You know Wernicke, surely?" Curiously, none of them did. I described the moment when his widow threw a plate at me, just like that, in her living room, it hit me on the shoulder, and it hurt quite a lot. Wives, I explained, were the absolute nightmare for any biographer, and one of the reasons this new job was such a pleasure to me was the absence of . . . well, you know!

Kaminski moved his hand, and as if on command, everyone stood up. We went out onto the terrace. The sun was sinking on the horizon, and the mountainsides glowed dark red. "Amazing," said Mrs. Clure, and her husband stroked her gently across the shoulders. I finished the wine in my glass and looked around for someone to refill it. I felt pleasantly tired. I should really go home now and replay the tapes with the conversations of the last two weeks. But I didn't feel like it. Maybe they'd invite me to spend the night up here. I went to stand next to Miriam and inhaled. "Chanel?"

"Excuse me?"

"Your perfume."

"What? No." She shook her head and moved away from me. "No!"

"You should leave while there's still light," said Bogovic.

"I'll be fine."

"You won't be able to find your way back!"

"Do you know that from experience?"

Bogovic grinned. "I never go anywhere on foot."

"The road isn't lit," said the banker.

"Someone could drive me," I proposed.

There was silence for a few seconds.

"The road isn't lit," the banker said again.

"He's right," said Kaminski hoarsely. "You need to start down."

"It's much safer," said Clure.

I held my glass tighter and looked from one to the next. They were silhouettes against the sunset. I cleared my throat, now was the moment when someone would have to ask me to stay. I cleared my throat again. "Well then . . . I'll be going."

"Follow the road," said Miriam. "After a kilometer or so there's a signpost, you go left and you'll be there in twenty minutes."

I glared at her, put the glass on the ground, buttoned my jacket, and set off. After a few steps, I heard them all burst out laughing behind me. I listened, but already I couldn't catch what they were saying; the wind carried only snatches of words. I was cold. I walked faster. I was glad to be out of there. Disgusting little brownnoses, repellent the way they sucked up to you! I felt sorry for the old man.

It really was getting dark very quickly. I had to narrow my eyes and squint to see where the road was going; I felt grass under my feet, stopped, and groped my way very carefully back onto the asphalt. In the valley, the pinpricks of streetlights were already visible. And here was the signpost, though it was too dark to read, and that must be the path I had to take.

I lost my footing and fell flat. I was so furious I

picked up a stone and flung it into the blackness of the valley. I rubbed my knee and imagined the stone collecting other stones as it fell, more and more of them until finally it turned into a rockslide that buried some innocent walker. The thought pleased me and I threw another stone. I wasn't sure if I was still on the path, I could feel the shale shifting under my feet, and almost fell again. I was cold. I bent down, groped around on the ground, and felt the hard-packed earth of the path. Should I just sit down and wait for daybreak? I might freeze, though not before I'd died of boredom, but either way it wouldn't be a fall that killed me.

No—out of the question! Blindly I set one foot in front of the other, inching forward by sheer willpower, clutching bushes as I went. Just as I was wondering whether I shouldn't in fact call for help, I saw something that formed itself into the contours of the wall of a house, and a steep roof. And then I could see windows, light glowing through closed curtains, and I was on a regular lit street. I came around a corner and found myself on the village square. Two men in leather jackets looked at me curiously, and a woman in curlers on the balcony of a hotel clutched a whimpering poodle to her bosom.

I pushed open the door to the Belview boarding-house and looked around for the proprietress, but

she was nowhere to be seen, the reception area was empty. I took my key and went upstairs to my room. My suitcase was next to my bed, the walls were hung with watercolors of cows, an Edelweiss, and a farmer with a shaggy white beard. My pants were filthy from the fall I'd taken and I didn't have another pair with me, but the mud could be brushed off. What I needed right now was a bath.

While the tub was filling, I unpacked my tape recorder, the satchel with the taped conversations, and the book with the complete images, *Manuel Kaminski, His Paintings*. I listened to the messages on my cell phone: Elke asked me to call back right away. The culture editor of the *Evening News* needed the Bahring hatchet job ASAP. Then Elke again: Sebastian, call me, it's important! Then a third time: Sebastian, *please*. I nodded, though I really wasn't paying attention, and switched off the phone.

In the bathroom mirror I eyed my naked self with a vague feeling of dissatisfaction. I set the book of collected Kaminski paintings down next to the tub. The foam made little popping sounds, and smelled pleasantly sweet. I slid slowly down into the water, lost my breath for a few moments because it was so hot, and felt I was swimming in a vast, motionless sea. Then I groped for the book.

III

FIRST THERE WERE the botched drawings of a twelve-year-old: humans with wings, birds with human heads, snakes, and swords swooping through the air: absolutely zero evidence of talent. And yet the great Richard Rieming, who had lived with Manuel's mother in Paris for two years, had used several of them to illustrate his volume of poetry *Roadside Words*. After war broke out, Rieming had to emigrate, found passage on a ship to America, and died of a lung infection during the voyage. Two childhood photographs of a chubby Manuel in a sailor suit, one of them showing him wearing glasses that grotesquely enlarged his eyes, the other one showing him blinking as if he couldn't tolerate bright light. Not a good-looking child. I turned the page, the paper swelling in the damp.

Now came the exercises in symbolism. He had painted hundreds of them, soon after leaving school and his mother's death, alone in a rented apartment, protected by his Swiss passport during the German occupation. Later he burned almost all of them, the few that survived were bad enough: gold backgrounds, clumsily painted falcons above trees with gloomy heads growing up out of them, a crudely rendered blowfly on a flower, looking as if it were made of cement. God knows what would have brought him to paint such a thing. For a moment, the book got away from me and sank into the foam; the glistening white seemed to climb up the paper, and I wiped it away. Taking a letter of recommendation from Rieming, he went to Nice to show his work to Matisse, but Matisse advised him to change his style, and, helpless, he went home again. A year after the end of the war, he visited the salt mines of Clairance, got separated from the guide, and wandered for hours through the empty passageways. After he'd been located and brought back out, he locked himself away for five days. Nobody knew what had gone on. But starting from then, he began to paint quite differently.

His friend and patron Dominik Silva paid for him to get a studio. There he worked, studied perspective, composition, and the theory of color, de-

stroyed all his sketches, began again from scratch, destroyed, began again. Two years later Matisse arranged his first exhibition at the Théophraste Renoncourt Gallery in Saint-Denis. That was where he showed for the first time (I was thumbing my way further) a new series of paintings: Reflections.

Today the series hung in the Metropolitan Museum in New York. The paintings were of mirrors that faced one another at different angles. Silvery gray passageways opened into infinity, slightly crooked, filled with otherworldly, cold light. Details of the frames or impurities on the glass multiplied and formed rows of identical copies that shrank away into the distance until they disappeared altogether out of the field of vision. A few of the pictures contained, as if by oversight, traces of the painter himself, a hand holding a brush, the corner of an easel, captured accidentally in one of the mirrors and repeated endlessly. Once a candle sparked a fire of dozens of flames licking upward together, another time the surface of a table stretched away, strewn with papers, and in one corner a postcard reproduction of Velázquez's Las Meninas, between two mirrors that met at right angles so that the reflection of one in the other produced a third mirror that instead of showing things in reverse showed them the right way around, creating a miraculously symmetrical

chaos: the effect was of enormous complexity. André
Breton wrote an ecstatic article, Picasso bought three
of them, it looked as if Kaminski was going to
become famous. But it didn't happen. Nobody knew
why; it just didn't happen. After three weeks the
exhibition ended, Kaminski took the paintings back
home with him and was as unknown as he'd been
before. Two photographs showed him with large
glasses that gave him something of the air of an
insect. He married Adrienne Nalle, the owner of a
successful paper business, and lived for fourteen
months in a certain comfort. Then Adrienne left him
with the newborn Miriam, and the marriage was
dissolved.

I turned on the hot-water tap; too much, I suppressed a cry, a little bit less, that's it. I propped the
book on the edge of the bath. There was a lot I
needed to talk to him about. When did he learn
about his eye disease? Why didn't the marriage hold
up? What had happened down in the mine? I had
other people's opinions on tape, but I needed quotes
from him himself, things he hadn't yet said to anyone. My book should not come out before his death
and not too long afterward either, for a short time it
would be at the center of all attention. I'd be invited
to go on TV, I would talk about him and at the bottom of the screen it would show my name and

biographer of Kaminski. This would get me a job with one of the big art magazines.

The book was now getting quite wet. I skipped over the rest of the *Reflections* and leafed to the smaller oil and tempera paintings of the next decade. He had lived alone again, Dominik Silva gave him money regularly, sometimes he sold a few paintings. His palette brightened, his line got crisper. Pushing to the very boundaries of the recognizable, he painted abstract landscapes, cityscapes, scenes of busy streets that dissolved into a viscous mist. A man walked along, pulling his own dissolving contours behind him, mountains were swallowed up in a pulp of clouds, a tower seemed to turn transparent under the fierce pressure of the background; you struggled in vain to see it clearly, but what had been a window a moment ago turned out to be a trick of the light, what had looked like artfully decorated stonework turned out to be a strangely shaped cloud, and the longer you looked, the less of the tower you found. "It's quite simple," said Kaminski in his first interview, "and damned difficult. Basically I'm going blind. That's what I paint. And that's all."

I leaned my head against the tiled wall and balanced the book on my chest. *Chromatic Light at Evening*, *Magdalena Daydreaming at Prayer*, and above all *Thoughts of a Sleepy Walker*, after Rieming's most famous poem: an

almost imperceptible human figure, wandering through a pewter-gray darkness. The *Walker*, apparently solely on the basis of Rieming's poem, was included in an exhibition on the Surrealists, where by chance it caught the eye of Claes Oldenburg. Two years later Oldenburg arranged for one of Kaminski's weakest works, *The Interrogation of St. Thomas*, to be shown in a Pop Art show at the Leo Castelli Gallery in New York. The title was expanded to include the tagline *painted by a blind man*, and the picture was hung next to a photo of Kaminski in dark glasses. When he was told about this, he got so angry that he took to his bed and ran a fever for two weeks. When he was able to get up again, he was famous.

I stretched out both arms cautiously and shook first my right hand, then the left; the book was quite heavy. Looking through the open door, my eyes fell on the picture of the old farmer. He was holding a scythe in his hands, looking at it proudly. I liked the thing. Actually, I liked it better than the pictures I had to write about every day.

Because of the rumors about his blindness, Kaminski's paintings suddenly went all around the world. And as his protests that he could still see gradually gained credence, it was too late. No way back. The Guggenheim Museum put on a retrospective, his prices shot up into the stratosphere, photos showed

him with his fourteen-year-old daughter, a really
pretty girl back then, at openings in New York, Mon-
treal, and Paris. But his eyes were getting steadily
worse. He bought a house in the Alps and disappeared from view.

Six years later Bogovic organized Kaminski's last
show in Paris. Twelve large-format paintings, once
again in tempera. Almost all bright colors, yellow
and light blue, a stinging green, transparent beiges;
streams of color that tangled and merged into one
another, yet, when you stepped back or narrowed
your eyes, suddenly were sheltering wide landscapes: hills, trees, fresh grass under summer rain, a
pale sun that dissolved the clouds into a milky haze.
I leafed more slowly. I liked them. A couple of them
kept me looking for a long time. The water slowly
grew cold.

But it was better not to like them, because the
critical reaction to them had been annihilating. They
were called kitsch, a painful blunder, evidence of his
illness. A last full-page photograph showed Kaminski
with a cane, dark glasses, and a strangely cheerful
expression, wandering through the rooms of the
gallery. Shivering with cold, I shut the book and laid
it down next to the tub. Only too late did I notice the
big puddle. I cursed: I couldn't sell it at the church
flea market in a state like that. I stood up, pulled out

the plug, and watched a little worm of water drain everything away. I looked in the mirror. Bald spot? No way.

Almost everyone I talked to about Kaminski reacted with astonishment that he was still alive. It seemed unbelievable that he should still exist, hidden in the mountains, in his large house, in the shadows of his blindness and his fame. That he should follow the same news that we did, listen to the same radio programs, was part of our world. I'd known for quite a while that it was time for me to write a book. My career had begun well, but now it was stagnating. First I had thought maybe I should do a polemic, an attack on a famous painter or movement; a total trashing of photorealism, maybe, or a defense of photorealism, but then suddenly photorealism was out of fashion. So why not write a biography? I hesitated between Balthus, Lucian Freud, and Kaminski, then the first of them died and the second was reported to be already in conversations with Bahring. I yawned, dried myself off, and put on my pajamas. The hotel telephone rang, I went into my bedroom, and picked up without thinking.

"We have to talk," said Elke.

"How did you get this number?"

"Who cares? We have to talk."

It must be really urgent. She was on a business trip for her advertising agency, and normally she never called when she was on the road.

"Not a good time. I'm very busy."

"Now!"

"Of course," I said, "hang on." I put down the receiver. In the darkness outside the window, I could make out the mountaintops and a pale half-moon. I breathed deeply in and out. "What is it?"

"I wanted to talk to you yesterday, but once again you managed to fix things so that you didn't get home till after I'd left. And now . . ."

I blew into the receiver. "There seems to be a bad connection."

"Sebastian, it's not a cell phone. There's nothing the matter with the connection."

"Excuse me," I said. "Just a moment."

I let the receiver sink down. I could feel the soft panic rising. I could guess what she wanted to say to me, and I absolutely must not allow myself to hear it. Just hang up? But I'd done that three times already. Hesitantly I raised the receiver again. "Yes?"

"It's about the apartment."

"Can I call you tomorrow? I've got a lot to do, I'll be back next week, then we can . . ."

"No you won't."

"What?"

"Come back. Not here. Sebastian, you don't live here anymore."

I cleared my throat. Now was the moment I needed an idea. Something simple and convincing. Now! But I couldn't think of anything.

"Back then you said it was only temporary. Just a few days, till you found something."

"And?"

"That was three months ago."

"There aren't many apartments."

"There are enough, and it can't go on like this."

I said nothing. Maybe that was the most effective tactic.

"Besides, I've been getting to know somebody."

I said nothing. What was she expecting? Should I cry, scream, plead? I was perfectly prepared to do all three. I thought of her apartment: the leather armchair, the marble table, the expensive couch. The wet bar, the stereo setup, and the big flat-screen TV. She'd really met someone who was willing to listen to her carrying on about the agency, vegetarian food, politics, and Japanese movies?

"I know it isn't easy," she said with a break in her voice. "I didn't want . . . to tell you over the phone. But there's no other way."

I said nothing.

"And you know it can't go on like this."

She'd said that already. But why not? I could see the living room in front of me: four hundred square feet, soft carpets, views of the park. On summer afternoons a gentle southern light played on the walls.

"I can't believe it," I said, "and I don't believe it."

"You have to. I've packed your things."

"What?"

"You can collect your suitcases. Or actually when I get back I'll have them delivered to you at the *Evening News.*"

"Not in the newsroom!" I cried. That was all I needed. "Elke, I'm going to forget this conversation. You didn't call and I haven't heard a word. We'll talk about it all next week."

"Walter says if you come back one more time, he's going to throw you out himself."

"Walter?"

She didn't reply. Did he have to be called Walter?

"He's moving in on Sunday," she said quietly.

Ah, now I got it: the apartment shortage was driving people to do the most astonishing things. "And where am I supposed to go?"

"I don't know. To a hotel. Or a friend."

A friend? The face of my tax accountant rose in front of me, followed by the face of someone I'd

been at school with, and whom I'd bumped into on the street the previous week. We'd shared a beer and hadn't known what to talk about. I spent the whole time racking my brains for his name.

"Elke, it's our apartment!"

"It isn't ours. Have you ever paid anything toward the rent?"

"I painted the bathroom."

"No, painters painted the bathroom. You just called them up. I paid."

"You're keeping count now?"

"Why not?"

"I can't believe it." Had I said that already? "I would never have believed you were capable of it."

"Yes, I know," she said. "Me neither. Me neither. How are you getting on with Kaminski?"

"We hit it off right away. I think he likes me. The daughter's a problem. She shields him from everything. I have to get rid of her somehow."

"I wish you all the best, Sebastian. Maybe you still have a chance."

"What does that mean?"

She didn't reply.

"Hang on. I want to know. What do you mean?"

She hung up.

I immediately dialed her cell phone, but she didn't answer. I tried again. A calm computer voice

invited me to leave a message. I tried again. And again. After the ninth attempt I gave up.

Suddenly the room didn't look so comfortable anymore. The pictures of the Edelweiss, the cows, and the wild-haired old farmer were vaguely threatening, the night outside too close and unsettling. Was this my future? Boardinghouses and sublet rooms, spying landladies, cooking smells at lunchtime, and the early-morning racket of unknown vacuum cleaners? It must not come to that!

The poor girl was completely off the wall, I almost felt sorry for her. If I knew her, she'd be regretting it already; by tomorrow at the latest she'd be calling me in tears to say she was sorry. She couldn't fool me. Already feeling a little calmer, I picked up the recorder, stuck in the first tape, and closed my eyes so as to be able to remember things better.

IV

"Who?"

"Kaminski. Manuel K-A-M-I-N-S-K-I. Did you know him?"

"Manuel. Yes, yes, yes." The old lady smiled expressionlessly.

"When was that?"

"Was what?"

She turned a waxy shriveled ear toward me. I leaned forward and screamed, "When!"

"My God! Thirty years."

"It must be over fifty."

"Not that many."

"Yes it is. You can count!"

"He was very serious. Dark. Always in the shadows, somehow. Dominik introduced us."

"Madam, what I actually wanted to ask . . ."

"Have you heard Pauli?" She pointed to a bird-cage. "He sings so beautifully. You're writing about all that?"

"Yes."

Her head drooped of its own accord, for a moment I thought she'd fallen asleep, but then she twitched and straightened herself up again. "He always said he'd be unknown for a long time. Then famous, then forgotten again. You're writing about all that? Then you should also write . . . that we had no idea."

"About what?"

"That you can get so old."

"What was your name again?"

"Sebastian Zollner."

"From the university?"

"Yes . . . from the university."

He sniffed audibly, his hand was heavy as he ran it over his bald spot. "Let me think. Got to know him? I asked Dominik who the arrogant guy was, he said Kaminski, as if it meant something. Maybe you know there had already been public performances of my compositions."

"Interesting," I said wearily.

"For the most part he just smiled away at nothing. Pompous ass. We all know people like that, who

think they're so important before they've ever done a thing . . . and then it all comes true, *mundus vult decipi*. I have worked on a symphony. I composed a quartet that was performed in Donaueschingen, and Ansermet said it was . . ."

I cleared my throat.

"Oh, Kaminski. That's why you're here. You're not here about me, you're here about him, I know. Once we were invited to look at his paintings, the ones Dominik Silva had at home, he had this apartment on the rue Verneuil. Kaminski himself used to sit in the corner and yawn, as if the whole thing were a bore. Maybe it was to him, I couldn't blame him. Tell me, what university are you actually from?"

"Did I understand correctly," asked Dominik Silva, "that you're paying for lunch?"

"Order whatever you like!" I said, surprised. Behind us, cars roared past heading toward the Place des Vosges, and waiters neatly snaked their way between the wicker chairs.

"Your French is good."

"It's okay."

"Manuel's French was always dreadful. I never met anyone with so little gift for languages."

"You weren't easy to find." He looked scrawny

and fragile, his nose jutting out against a face that was curiously collapsed in on itself.

"I live in different circumstances from the old days."

"You did a lot for Kaminski," I said carefully.

"Don't overestimate it. If I hadn't, someone else would. People like him always find people like me. He wasn't born rich. His father, who was Swiss of Polish parentage, or vice versa, I don't remember anymore, went into bankruptcy before Kaminski was born, and died, his mother was supported by Rieming later on, but Rieming didn't have much money either. Manuel always needed money."

"You paid his rent?"

"It happened."

"And today you're . . . no longer wealthy?"

"Times change."

"Where did you get to know him from?"

"Matisse. I visited him in Nice, he said there's a young painter in Paris, a protégé of Richard Rieming."

"And his pictures?"

"Nothing earth-shattering. But I thought, this will change."

"Why?"

"Because of him, really. He simply gave you the impression that he could go places. At the beginning,

his stuff was fairly bad, overloaded Surrealism. That all changed with Therese." His lips rubbed together; I wondered if he still had any teeth in his head. On the other hand, he'd just ordered a steak.

"You mean Adrienne," I said.

"I know who I mean. Maybe this will surprise you, but I'm not senile. Adrienne came later."

"Who was Therese?"

"My God, she was everything! She changed him completely, even if he would never admit it. You've certainly heard about his experience in the salt mine, he talks about it often enough."

"That's where I'm going the day after tomorrow."

"Do whatever you want. But Therese was more important."

"I didn't know."

"Then you need to start at the beginning again."

"Let's be candid. Do you consider him a great painter?"

"Yes, of course." I returned Professor Komenev's stare. "Within bounds."

Komenev folded his hands behind his head, and his chair tipped right back in a single movement. His little fuzzy beard stuck out straight from his chin. "Okay, to take things in order. No need to

waste words on the early pictures. Then the *Reflections*. Very unusual for that time. Technically brilliant. But still rather sterile. A good basic idea, too often worked through too exactly and too precisely, and the Old Master stuff with the tempera doesn't make it any better. A little bit too much Piranesi. Then *Chromatic Light*, the *Walker*, the street scenes. At first sight, fabulous. But not exactly subtle, thematically speaking. And let's be honest, if people didn't know about him going blind . . ." He shrugged. "You've seen the pictures themselves?"

I hesitated. I had thought about flying to New York, but it was quite expensive and besides—what were art books for? "Of course."

"Then you will have noticed the uncertain brush-work. He must have used strong magnifying glasses. No comparison to the earlier technical perfection. And after that? Oh God, the verdict is already in. Calendar art! Have you seen the hideous dog on the beach, the Goya knockoff?"

"So, first too much technique and too little feeling, then the reverse."

"You could say that." He lifted his hands from behind his neck, the chair tipped upright again. "Two years ago I discussed him again in a seminar. The kids were baffled. He had nothing to say to them anymore."

"Did you ever meet him?"

"No, why would I? When my *Some Thoughts on Kaminski* came out, I sent him the book. He never responded. Didn't think it mattered! As I say, he's a good painter, and good painters are transient. Only great painters are not."

"You should have gone there," I said.

"Excuse me?"

"It's pointless to write and then sit there waiting for an answer. You have to go there. You have to take him by surprise. When I wrote my portrait of Wernicke—you know Wernicke?"

He looked at me, puzzled.

"It had just happened and his family didn't want to talk to me. But I didn't leave. I stood at their front door and told them I was going to write about his suicide anyway, and the only choice they had was whether to talk to me or not. 'If you choose not to,' I said, 'what that means is that your own views won't be represented. But if you were prepared . . .'"

"Excuse me." Komenev leaned forward and stared at me. "What exactly are you talking about?"

"It didn't last that long. A year, and then the thing with Therese was over."

The waiter brought the steak with roast potatoes, Silva grabbed his knife and fork and began to eat, his throat quivering as he swallowed. I ordered another Coca-Cola.

"She was really something special. She never saw him as he was, but as what he could become. And then that's what she made him. I can still remember how she looked at one of his pictures and said, quite quietly, 'Do those always have to be eagles?' You should have heard the way she said 'eagles.' That was the end of his Symbolist phase. She was wonderful! The marriage to Adrienne was just a messed-up mirror image, she looked a little like Therese. Need I say more? If you ask me, he never got over her. If every life has one decisive catastrophe"—he shrugged his shoulders—"then that was his."

"But his daughter is Adrienne's?"

"When she was thirteen, her mother died." He stared into nowhere, as if the memory were painful. "Then she came to him in this house at the end of the world, and since then she has taken care of everything." He pushed a chunk of meat that was a bit too ambitious into his mouth, and there was a pause before he was able to speak again; I made an effort not to look. "Manuel always found the people he needed. He felt the world owed him."

"Why did Therese leave him?"

He didn't answer. Maybe he was hard of hearing. I pushed the recorder closer to him. "Why . . .?"

"How do I know? Mr. Zollner, there are always a thousand explanations, a thousand versions of everything, and in the end, the truth is always the most banal. No one knows what happened, and no one has any idea of what someone else thinks of them! We should stop. I'm no longer accustomed to people listening to me."

I looked at him in astonishment. His nose was trembling, he'd laid down his knife and fork, and was looking at me with swollen eyes. What had upset him? "I had a few more questions," I said cautiously.

"Don't you understand? We're talking about him as if he were already dead."

"One time a new piece was being put on." He sat up straight, rubbed his bald spot, then ran a hand over his double chin and rumpled his forehead. Start up one more time with your compositions, I thought, and I'm going to shove this recorder straight down your throat!

"He came to the opening night with Therese Lessing. An exceptionally intelligent woman, God knows what she saw in him . . . it was the best sort

of avant-garde, a sort of Black Mass, blood-smeared performers, dumb show under an upturned cross, but the two of them laughed the whole time. First they tittered and destroyed everyone else's concentration, then they started laughing out loud. Until they got thrown out. The atmosphere was all gone to hell, or rather not gone to hell, if you see what I mean, anyhow, the whole thing was over. After Therese's death he got married, and after his wife, not unnaturally, went off with Dominik, I didn't see him again."

"With Dominik?"

"You don't know that?" He frowned, his eyebrows shot up in a thicket, his chin twitched. "What kind of research are you doing? He never came to my concerts, they didn't interest him. A time like that never comes twice. Ansermet wanted to conduct my symphonic *Suite*, but it never happened, because . . . what, already? Stay, I have a couple of interesting LPs. You'll never hear them anywhere else!"

"What do you think of his pictures?" Professor Mehring looked at me watchfully over the frames of his glasses.

"First, too much technique and too little feeling," I said. "Then the reverse."

"That's what Komenev says too. But I think it's wrong."

"So do I," I said hastily. "A prejudice, and a bad one."

"And Komenev talked completely differently twenty years ago. But Kaminski was in fashion back then. I discussed him in class a year ago. The students were riveted. I also think his late work is being misjudged. That will correct itself in time."

"You were his assistant?"

"Only briefly. I was nineteen, my father knew Bogovic, he arranged things. I was responsible for grinding the pigments. He had the idea that he'd get more intense colors if we did it ourselves. If you ask me, pure chutzpah. But I was allowed to live upstairs in his house, and if you want to know the truth, I was sort of in love with his daughter. She was so beautiful, and basically she never saw anybody aside from him. But she wasn't very interested in me."

"Were you with him when he was painting?"

"He needed to use big magnifying glasses, he fastened them to his head like a jeweler. He was pretty high-strung, sometimes he broke his brush in sheer rage, and when he felt I was being too slow . . . well, it's hard for us to imagine what he had to go through. He had planned every painting in detail, made whole series of sketches, but when it came

time to mix the paints, he couldn't get things to come out the way he wanted. After a month I quit."

"Are you still in touch with him?"

"I send Christmas cards."

"Does he reply?"

"Miriam replies. I assume that's as far as I'll ever get."

"I've only got ten minutes." Bogovic stroked his beard uneasily. The window looked onto the walls of the Palais Royal, a sketch by David Hockney of a California villa hung over the desk. "All I can say is I love him like a father. Go ahead, make sure you've got that on tape. A father. I got to know him at the end of the sixties, Papa was still running the gallery, he was so proud that Kaminski had become one of his artists. In those days, Manuel came by train, he didn't fly. But he loves to take trips. He's gone on long journeys, of course he needs someone to drive him. He likes adventures! We handled his great landscape paintings. Probably the best things he ever did. The Pompidou almost bought two of them."

"What went wrong?"

"Nothing, they just didn't buy them. Mr. Zellner, I have . . ."

"Zollner!"

". . . known many creative people in my lifetime. Good people. But only one genius."

The door opened, an assistant wearing a tight blouse came in and laid a message in front of him; Bogovic looked at it for a few seconds, then set it aside. I looked at her and smiled, she looked away, but still I could tell she liked me. She was adorably shy. As she went out, I leaned unobtrusively to one side, so that she had to brush against me as she passed, but she evaded me. I winked at Bogovic, he frowned. He must be gay.

"I go see him twice a year," he said, "next week is when I'm due to go again. Strange that he really took himself out of circulation. Papa would have gotten him an apartment here or in London. But that's not what he wanted."

"Is he totally blind?"

"If you find out, do let me know! He hasn't been doing so well recently, major bypass operation. I was there myself, at the hospital . . . no, that's not right, I was there when Papa had the same thing. But I'd have done the same for him. As I said, I love this man. I didn't love my father. Manuel Kaminski is the greatest. Sometimes I think"—he pointed to the picture of the villa—"David is the greatest. Or Lucian or whoever. Sometimes I even think I'm the greatest.

But then I think of him, and I know we're nothing."
He pointed to a painting on the opposite wall: a
bowed figure sat on the coast of a dark ocean, beside
it stood a huge dog, twisted peculiarly out of perspective. "You know this one, don't you? *Death by the
Faded Sea.* This I will never sell."

I realized Komenev had mentioned this painting.
Or was it Mehring? I couldn't remember what had
been said and if I was supposed to like the thing or
not. "Doesn't look like Kaminski," I said before I had
time to think.

"In what way?"

"Because he . . . because . . ." I stared at the
palms of my hands. "Because . . . of the brushwork.
You know, the brushwork. What do you know about
Therese Lessing?"

"Never heard the name."

"How good a negotiator is he?"

"Miriam does all that. She started when she was
seventeen. She's better than a lawyer and a wife com-
bined."

"She never married."

"And?"

"She's been living with him for such a long time.
Up there in the mountains, cut off from everything.
Right?"

"Mmmm," he said coolly. "Now you must excuse me. Maybe next time you should make an appointment instead of just . . ."

"Of course!" I got to my feet. "I'll be there next week too. He's invited me." Bogovic's handshake was soft and a little damp. "To Arcadia!"

"To where?"

"When I'm rich, I'm going to buy *Death by the Faded Sea* from you. No matter what the price is."

He looked at me wordlessly.

"Just kidding!" I said happily. "No harm intended. It was a joke."

"Haven't a clue what the old idiot said to you. I never lived with Adrienne."

It hadn't been easy to persuade Silva to meet me again; I'd had to emphasize repeatedly that he could choose where we were to eat. He shook his head, his lips were smeared all brown with chocolate ice cream, not a pretty sight.

"I liked her and I felt sorry for her. I took care of her and the child, because Manuel didn't want to anymore. Maybe he took it badly. But that's all that happened."

"Who am I supposed to believe now?"

"That's your problem, nobody owes you an accounting!" He looked up at me. "You'll meet Manuel quite soon. But you won't be able to imagine what he was back then. He managed to convince everyone that he was going to be great one day. One had to give him what he wanted. Therese was the only one who didn't . . ." He scraped the last drops of ice cream out of the glass and licked both sides of the spoon. "Only Therese." He thought for a bit, but seemed to have forgotten what it was he wanted to say.

"Would you like a coffee?" I asked uneasily. The whole thing was already way over my own spending limit; I hadn't yet had a conversation with Megelbach about expenses.

"Mr. Zollner, this is all old history! In reality, none of us exists anymore. Old age is absurd. You're here and you're not here, like a ghost." For a few seconds he stared past me out at the roofs, and the other side of the street. His neck was so thin that the veins stood out clearly. "Miriam was very gifted, alive, a little hot-tempered. When she was twenty, she had a fiancé. He came to visit, stayed for two days, left, and never came back. It's not easy to have him for a father. I would like to see her again."

"I'll tell her."

"Better not." He smiled softly.

"I'd like to ask another few questions."

"Believe me, so would I."

"That we didn't know anyone could get so old—write that! You have to write that!" She pointed at the birdcage. "Do you hear Pauli?"

"Did you know Therese well?"

"When she died, he wanted to kill himself."

"Really?" I sat up straight.

Her eyes closed for a moment: even her eyelids were wrinkled, I'd never seen such wrinkles before. "That's what Dominik said. I would never have asked Manuel about it. Nobody would. But he was completely beside himself. It was only when Dominik told him she was dead that he stopped searching for her. Would you like tea?"

"No. Yes. Yes please. Do you have a photo of her?"

She lifted the teapot and poured shakily. "Ask her, maybe she'll send you one."

"Who should I ask?"

"Therese."

"But she's dead!"

"No, no, she lives up north, on the coast."

"She didn't die?"

"No, that's just what Dominik said. Manuel would

never have stopped trying to find her. I liked her husband, Bruno, very much. He was such a fine human being, quite different from . . . do you take sugar? He's been dead a long time now. Most everybody's dead." She put down the teapot. "Milk?"

"No! Do you have her address?"

"I think I do. Listen, do you hear him? He sings so beautifully. Canaries don't often sing. Pauli's an exception."

"Please give me her address!" She didn't answer, she seemed not to have understood me.

"To be honest," I said slowly, "I don't hear a thing."

"What?"

"He's not singing, he's not moving, and I don't think he's actually doing that well. Please would you give me the address?"

V

Shortly after ten I was woken by the sun shining in through the window. I was lying on top of the bedclothes, surrounded by a dozen audiocassettes, the tape recorder had landed on the floor. In the distance I could hear church bells. I dragged myself out of bed.

I had breakfast under the same stag's head I'd seen through the window the day before. The coffee tasted like water, at the next table a father was being mean to his son, and the little boy let his head drop, closed his eyes, and pretended he wasn't there. Hugo crawled over the carpet with his ears held flat against his head. I called the proprietress over and said the coffee was undrinkable. She nodded indifferently and brought a new pot. I should think so, I said. She shrugged. The coffee was actually stronger, three

cups of it and my heart was pounding. I shouldered my bag and set out.

The path I had come down last night seemed fairly broad and harmless by light of day, and the steep slope had turned itself into a gently slanting meadow full of flowers. Two cows looked at me mournfully, a man with a scythe, who looked like the old farmer in the picture, called out something incomprehensible, I nodded at him, he laughed and made a gesture as if he were throwing something away. The air was cool, and yesterday's sultriness had dissipated. When I reached the signpost I was barely out of breath.

I went up the road at a fast pace, after barely ten minutes I saw the parking area and the houses. The little tower poked up into the sky. The gray BMW was sitting in front of the garden gate. I rang.

This wasn't a good moment, said Anna aggressively. Mr. Kaminski wasn't feeling well, he didn't even say good night to his guests last night.

"That's bad," I said, reassured.

Yes, she said, very bad. Please come back tomorrow.

I walked past her through the hall and the dining room onto the terrace and squeezed my eyes almost closed: the semicircle of mountains, framed in the glistening morning light. Anna came after me and

asked if I hadn't understood her. I told her I pre-
ferred to speak to Miss Kaminski. She stared at me,
then wiped her hands on her apron and went into
the house. I sat down on a garden chair and closed
my eyes. The sun's warmth was soft against my
cheek, I'd never breathed such clean air.

No, that wasn't right, I had once already. In
Clairance. I tried without success to push the memory away.

I had attached myself to a group of tourists
around four in the afternoon. The steel cage headed
down with a groaning noise, women laughed hys-
terically, ice-cold air came blowing up out of the
depths. For a few seconds there was total darkness.

A narrow passageway, electric lamps with a yel-
lowish light, a fire door made of steel that screamed
as it opened and closed. "Ne vous perdez pas, don't
get lost!" The leader shuffled forward ahead of us,
an American took photos, a woman touched the
white veins in the stone with curiosity. The air tasted
of salt. This was where Kaminski had got lost fifty
years ago.

The leader opened a steel door, we went around a
corner. It must have had to do with his eyes, I closed
mine for a moment and groped my way forward
blindly. The scene was important for my book: I
imagined I was Kaminski, tapping my way ahead,

blinking, touching, calling, finally standing still and calling out for so long that I knew nobody would ever hear me. I must be sure to crank up the prose for this episode as drastically as I could, I needed to get a first-serial deal in one of the major color magazines. Some idiot banged into me, I muttered a curse, he did the same, someone else groped my elbow, it was incredible how careless people could be but I withstood the temptation to open my eyes. I absolutely had to be able to describe the echo of his voice in the silence. It would work really well. "The echo in the silence," I said quietly. I heard people going off to the left. I let go of the wall, took a couple of cautious steps, found the wall on the other side, and followed them. Or followed the voices: after a time I was getting the feel of it. A door banged shut, and out of sheer reflex I opened my eyes. I was alone.

A short passageway, lit by three lamps. I was surprised that the door was more than thirty feet away, it had sounded so close. I hurried over and opened it. More lamps here, and metal pipes running along the low ceiling. No people.

I went back to the other end of the passageway. So they must have gone right, not left, and I'd misheard. My breath rose in little clouds. I reached the door. It was locked.

I wiped my forehead, in spite of the chill I felt hot. Okay, go back to the fork in the passage, then left again, back the way we'd come. I stood still, held my breath, listened: no voices. Nothing. I had never heard such a silence. I hurried along the passageway, reached the next fork, and hesitated. Had we come from the right? Yes, from the right. So now I must turn left. The steel door opened without resistance. Lamps, pipes, another fork, not a human being in sight. I'd gone the wrong way.

I had to laugh.

I went back to the last fork and turned left. Yet another door, but there was no light in the passageway behind it, it was filled with a darkness more complete than any that existed up on the earth's surface, in fright I slammed the door shut. The next group must be due to be flushed through soon, and then there must be workers down here, the mine was still operating as a business, after all. I listened. I cleared my throat and yelled; I was astonished to discover that there was no echo. The stone seemed to swallow my voice.

I turned off to the right, went through one, two, three doors in a straight line, the fourth was locked. Think logically! I went left, on through two steel doors, and found myself at a crossroads. According to what the guide had said, the doors were to pre-

vent draft in case a fire broke out; without them one single flame could suck all the air in the mine toward itself. Were there fire alarms? For a moment I played with the idea of lighting something. But I had nothing combustible with me, I'd even run out of cigarettes.

I noticed that tiny condensed drops of water were hanging off the pipes. Was that normal? I tried two doors, one was locked, the other led into a passageway I'd already been in before. Or had I? I wished I had a cigarette. I sat down on the ground.

Someone would come, would come soon, no doubt about it. The mine complex couldn't be all that large. Did they turn out the lights at night? The ground was as cold as ice, I couldn't stay sitting. I stood up. I called out. I called louder. I realized it wasn't doing any good. I yelled until I was hoarse.

I sat down again. An idiotic impulse made me pull out my cell phone, but of course there was no reception, you couldn't find anywhere more perfect for blocking reception than a salt mine. Hard to decide: was my situation merely painful, or was it dangerous? I leaned my head against the wall, for a second I thought I saw a spider, but it was just a little stain, there were no insects down here. I looked at my watch, an hour had already gone by, either time down here was going faster or my life was going

slower, or maybe my watch just wasn't keeping time properly. Should I go farther or wait here? I was suddenly tired. For just a moment, I closed my eyes.

I examined the veins in the rock. They ran toward one another, joined, but never crossed, just like the branches of a river. A never-ending slow torrent of salt in the bowels of the earth. I must not go to sleep, I thought, then I heard voices talking to me, which I answered, a piano was playing somewhere, then I was sitting in an airplane, looking at broad, glowing landscapes: mountains, towns, and a distant sea, people walked past, a child laughed, I looked at my watch, but my eyes couldn't focus on it properly. Standing up was an effort, my body was numb with cold. The steel door opened of its own accord, I went through it, found myself in Elke's living room, and knew that I was expected at last. She came toward me, I flung my arms wide in joy, and opened my eyes, I was sitting on the ground, under the wet pipes, in the yellow light of the underground lamps, alone.

It was a little after six. I'd been here two hours already. I was trembling with cold. I stood up, hopped from one foot to the other, and clapped my hands. I went to the end of the gallery, turned right, then left, then right, then left again. Then I stopped and pressed my hands against the rock.

How massive it felt. I leaned my forehead against it and tried to acquaint myself with the thought that I was going to die. Should I write something down, a last message for—who, actually? I sank to my knees, a hand landed hard on my shoulder. A tour guide with a big mustache, and behind him a dozen people with helmets, cameras, camcorders. "Monsieur, qu'est-ce vous faites là?"

I stood up, murmured something, rubbed away my tears, and fell in with the tourists. Two Japanese looked at me curiously, the guide opened a door: a babble of voices broke over me, the gallery was full of people. There was a souvenir stand selling postcards, lumps of the salt rock, and slides of milky salt lakes. An EXIT sign pointed to a staircase, a few minutes later the iron cage was cranking me noisily back up to ground level.

"You weren't supposed to come till tomorrow!"

I lifted my head. Miriam Kaminski was silhouetted in front of me in a nimbus of sunshine. Her black hair was shot through with fine lines of light.

"I just wanted to say hello."

"Hello. I'm leaving in an hour and I'll be back tomorrow."

"I'd hoped I could speak to your father."

She looked at me as if she hadn't heard right. "My

father isn't feeling well. Go for a walk, Mr. Zollner. Explore a little. It's worth the effort."

"Where are you going?"

"We're establishing a Kaminski Foundation. I'll be glad to explain the details, it could be of interest for your book."

"Absolutely." I understood: as long as she was there, I would not be able to speak to him alone. I nodded slowly, she avoided my eyes. It was natural that I would have a certain effect on her. Who knows, if I weren't someone she considered danger- ous . . . But nothing I could do about that. I stood up. "Then I'll go exploring."

I went quickly into the house, I had to make absolutely sure she didn't see me out. The kitchen door was almost closed, behind it there was the clat- ter of plates. I looked through the crack, Anna was in the process of washing dishes.

As I came in, she looked at me expression- lessly. Her hair was gathered into a thick plait, her apron was dirty, and her face was as round as a cart- wheel.

"Anna!" I said. "May I call you Anna?"

She shrugged her shoulders.

"I'm Sebastian. Call me Sebastian. The food yes- terday was wonderful. Can we talk?"

She didn't answer. I pulled up a stool, then pushed it away again and sat on the kitchen table. "Anna, isn't there something you want to do?"

She stared at me.

"I mean, that . . . you could do today. Yes?"

Through the window I saw the banker who'd been at last night's dinner come out of the house next door. He crossed the parking area, hooked his car key out of his pocket, opened the driver's door, and climbed in laboriously.

"Let me put it another way. Whatever you'd like to do today, I'd . . . no, let's say . . ."

"Two hundred," she said.

"What?"

"Just how dumb are you?" She looked at me calmly. "Two hundred, and I'll be away until midday tomorrow."

"That's a lot," I said hoarsely.

"Two hundred and fifty."

"You can't do that!"

"Three hundred."

"Two hundred," I said.

"Three hundred and fifty."

I nodded.

She held out her hand, I brought out my briefcase and counted out the money. I never normally carried

so much around with me; that was the sum I'd hoped would cover the whole trip.

"Okay, let's do it!" she said. Her skin had an oily sheen. She seized the money, her hand was so large that the bills disappeared into it. "My sister will call this afternoon, then I'll say I have to go to her at once. Tomorrow at noon I'll be back here."

"And not a minute earlier!" I said.

She nodded. "Now go."

My legs were a little wobbly as I went to the front door. All that money! But I'd gotten what I wanted. And God knows I had set it up pretty cleverly, she hadn't had a chance against me. I slowly set down the briefcase and leaned against the wall.

"Mr. Zollner!"

I whirled around.

"Lost your way?" asked Miriam.

"No, no—I just wanted . . ."

"I wouldn't want you to have any wrong impression," said Miriam. "We're glad about what you're doing."

"Thank you, I know."

"Things aren't easy right now. He's ill. Often he's like a child. But your book is very important to him."

I nodded sympathetically.

"When is it supposed to come out?"

I jumped. Did she suspect? "That's not settled yet."

"Why isn't it settled? Mr. Megelbach didn't want to tell me either."

"It depends on so many factors. On . . ." I shrugged. "Factors. A lot of factors. As soon as possible!"

She looked at me thoughtfully, I hastily said good-bye, and set off. This time the descent seemed to go very quickly: everything smelled of grass and flowers, an airplane swam lazily through the blue; I felt cheerful and almost weightless. I got money from an ATM and a new shaver in the village drugstore.

I went up to my room in the boardinghouse and looked at the old farmer on the wall, whistling to myself and drumming my fingers on my knee. I must have been a little nervous. I lay down on the bed without taking off my shoes, and stared at the ceiling for a while. Then I stood in front of the mirror and stayed like that for so long that my reflection became a stranger and looked absurd. I shaved and took a long shower. Then I reached for the receiver and dialed a number by heart. It rang five times before anyone picked up.

"Miss Lessing," I said, "it's me again, Sebastian Zollner. Don't hang up!"

"No!" said a high voice. "No!"

"Please, all I ask is that you listen to me!"

She hung up. For a few seconds I listened to the busy signal, then I dialed again.

"Zollner again. Please would you give me a short . . ."

"No!" She hung up.

I cursed. Nothing for it, it really did look as if I would have to drive up there myself. Which was all I needed!

In a restaurant on the main square, I ordered a miserable tuna fish salad. Tourists all around me, children crowing, fathers thumbing through maps, mothers sticking forks into huge portions of cake. The waitress was young and not hideous, I called after her: too much oil in the salad, please take it away again. She'd be glad to, she said, but I'd have to pay for it anyway. But I'd eaten almost none of it, I said. That was my affair, she said. I asked to see the proprietor. She said he wouldn't be there until the evening, but I could wait. As if I had nothing better to do, I said, and winked at her. I ate the salad, but when I wanted to pay my bill, it was a broad-shouldered colleague of hers who brought it. I left no tip.

I bought cigarettes and asked a young man for a light. We fell to talking: he was a student, visiting his parents during the vacation. What was he studying?

Art history, he said, looking at me a little defensively. Very understandable, I said, particularly if one comes from here. What did I mean? I gestured toward the slope of the mountain. God? Hardly, I said, great painters made their homes here. He didn't understand. Kaminski! He looked blank.

Did he really not know Kaminski? No, he didn't. The last pupil of Matisse, champion of the classical . . . He didn't concern himself with that sort of stuff, he interrupted me, his thing was contemporary art from the Alps. Full of exciting trends, you know, Gamraunig, and Göschl, of course, and Wagreiner. Who? Wagreiner, he said loudly, his face going pink. I didn't know Wagreiner? Really? He was only painting now with milk and edible substances. Why, I asked. He nodded, he was hoping for that one. Nietzsche.

Anxiously, I took a step back. Was Wagreiner a Neo-dadaist? He shook his head. Or a performance artist? No, no, no. Had I really never even heard of Wagreiner? I shook my head. He muttered something I couldn't catch and we eyed each other mistrustfully. Then we went our separate ways.

I went into the boardinghouse, packed my suitcase, and settled my bill. I would simply come back tomorrow, no reason to pay for a night when I

wouldn't be there. I nodded at the proprietress, threw away my cigarette, found the footpath, and started climbing. I didn't need any taxi, it was easy for me now, even though I had the suitcase to carry, I was soon up at the signpost. Up the road, first bend, second bend, third bend, then the parking area. The BMW was still standing in front of the garden gate. I rang, Anna opened the door immediately.

"Nobody home?"

"Only him."

"Why is the car still here?"

"She took the train."

I looked her straight in the eyes. "I've come, because I forgot my bag."

She nodded, went inside, and left the door open. I followed her.

"My sister called," she said.

"Really!"

"She needs help."

"If you want to go, I can stay with him."

She inspected me for a few seconds. "That would be kind."

"Think nothing of it."

She smoothed her apron, bent down, and picked up a well-stuffed overnight case. She went to the door, hesitated, and looked at me questioningly.

"No worries!" I said softly.

She nodded, breathed audibly in and out, then closed the door behind her. Through the kitchen window I watched her as she walked across the parking area with small, heavy steps. The bag swung in her hand.

VI

I STOOD IN THE HALL, ears cocked. To my left was the front door, to my right the dining room, and straight ahead the staircase went up to the second floor. I cleared my throat, my voice echoing oddly in the silence.

I went into the dining room. The windows were closed, the air stale. A fly was banging against a pane. I carefully opened the top drawer of the chest of drawers: tablecloths, neatly folded. The next one: knives, forks, and spoons. The bottom one: twenty years' worth of old magazines, *Life, Time, Paris-Match,* all jumbled together. The old wood resisted; I almost couldn't close the drawers. I went back into the hall.

To my left were four doors. I opened the first: a little room with a bed, table, and chair, a TV, a picture of the Madonna and a photo of the young Marlon

Brando. It must be Anna's room. Behind the next door was the kitchen, the one after that was the room where I'd been received the day before. The last one opened onto a staircase going down.

I took my bag and groped for the light switch. A single bulb cast its dirty light onto wooden steps, which creaked, and their downward pitch was so steep that I had to hang on to the banister. I hit another switch, spotlights crackled as they sprang to life, and I squeezed my eyes tight shut. When I'd gotten used to the glare, I realized I was in the studio.

A windowless space, lit only by four spotlights. Whoever had worked here hadn't needed any natural light. In the middle was an easel with a painting in its genesis; dozens of brushes were scattered over the floor. I bent down to feel them: all of them were dry. There was also a palette, the colors on it were hard as stone and cracked. I sucked in a mouthful of air: a normal cellar smell, a little damp, a faint odor of mothballs, no hint of paints or turpentine. Nobody had painted here for a long time.

The canvas on the easel was almost untouched, only three brushstrokes cut across its whiteness. They began in the same spot down on the left and then pulled apart, in the top right was a tiny field crosshatched in chalk. No sketching, nothing to indicate what should have grown out of this. As I

stepped back, I noticed that I had four shadows, one from each spotlight, that cut across one another at my feet. Several large canvases, covered with sail-cloth tarps, leaned against the wall.

I pulled the first tarp away and winced. Two eyes, a twisted mouth: a face, curiously distorted, like a reflection in flowing water. It was painted in bright colors, red lines pulled away from him like dying flames, his eyes as they observed me were questioning and cold. And although the style was unmistakable—the thin layer of color, the preference for red-yellow, which both Komenev and Mehring had written about—it looked utterly different from anything else of his I knew. I looked for his signature and didn't find it. I reached for the next cloth; as soon as I touched it, it emitted a cloud of dust.

The same face, this time a little smaller, more of a ball, a slightly contemptuous smile playing in the corners of the mouth. On the next canvas there it was again, this time with the mouth stretched unnaturally wide, the eyebrows angled violently toward the nose. The forehead was creased into masklike folds, and individual hairs straggled thinly, like tears in paper. No beginnings of a neck, no body, just the detached head floating in empty space. I pulled away tarp after tarp, and the face was becoming more and more deformed: the chin stretched

and lengthened, the colors became harsher, the forehead and ears grotesquely extended. But each time his eyes seemed more distant, indifferent, and, I pulled the tarp away, more filled with contempt. Now it was bulging outward as if in a funhouse mirror, had a Harlequin's nose and puckered frown lines, on the next canvas—the tarp got caught, I tore it off by full force, dust swirled up, making me sneeze—it crumpled together, as if a puppeteer were clenching his fist. On the canvas after that it was a hint of itself, seen in a blur through driving snow— the remaining paintings were unfinished, just sketches with a few patches of color, a forehead here, a cheek there. In the corner, as if thrown away, lay a sketch block. I picked it up, wiped it off, and opened it. The same face, from above, from below, from every side, even once, like a mask, seen from inside. The sketches were done in charcoal, increasingly unsure, the lines became shaky and missed one another. Finally there was more of a thick patch of pure black. Tiny splinters of charcoal trickled down at me. The remaining pages were empty.

I set aside the sketch block and began to search the paintings for a signature or a date. In vain. I turned one of the canvases around to examine its wooden stretchers, and a shard of glass fell onto the floor. I picked it up with the tips of my fingers. There

were more; the entire floor behind the pictures was carpeted in broken glass. I held the shard up to the spotlight and closed one eye: the light jumped a tiny distance, and its black housing bulged. The glass had been ground.

I got the camera out of my bag. A very good little Kodak, a Christmas present from Elke. The spotlights were so bright that I wouldn't need either a tripod or a flash. A painting, the photo editor of the *Evening News* had explained to me, must be photographed head-on, to avoid any foreshortening of perspective, if it is to be usable for reproduction. I photographed each canvas twice and then, standing back up and propping myself against the wall, the easel, the brushes on the floor, the shards of glass. I kept clicking till the memory card was full. Then I put the camera back in the bag and began to cover the paintings again.

It was hard work, and the tarps kept on getting hooked on things. Where did I know this face from? I started to hurry: I didn't know why, but I wanted to get out of here as quickly as possible. How in the world could it be familiar to me? I got to the last painting, met its contemptuous stare, and covered it up. I tiptoed to the door, switched off the light, and let out my breath involuntarily.

I stood in the hall again, ears cocked. The fly was still buzzing in the living room. "Hello?" Nobody answered. "Hello?" I went up to the second floor.

Two doors to the right, two to the left, one at the end of the landing. I began on the left. I knocked, waited for a moment, and opened the door.

It must be Miriam's room. A bed, a TV set, bookshelves, and a Kaminski, one of the *Reflections* series: three mirrors—at their center a discarded duster, a shoe, and a pencil, arranged as a parody of a still life—that organized themselves into a perfect system of surfaces; if you looked at it out of the corner of your eye, it seemed to shimmer faintly. It must be worth a fortune. I looked in the cupboards, but they held nothing but clothes, shoes, hats, a few pairs of glasses, silk underwear. I let one of the pairs of panties slide slowly through my fingers; I'd never met a woman who wore silk underwear. The drawer of the night table was filled with boxes of medications: Baldrian, Valium, Benedorm, various kinds of sleeping pills and tranquilizers. The instruction leaflets would have made interesting reading, but I didn't have time.

Next door was a bathroom. Pristine, smelling of cleaning stuff, there was a sponge, still damp, lying in the tub, and three perfume bottles in front of the

mirror. One of them was Chanel. No shaver, so the old man must use another bathroom. How did blind people shave, anyway?

The door at the end of the passage led into an unaired room. The windows hadn't been cleaned, the cupboards were bare, the bed wasn't made: an unused guest room. A little spider sent a tremor across the web she'd spun over the windowsill. On the table was a pencil with an almost-worn-down eraser and teeth marks in the wood. I picked it up, rolled it between my fingers, put it back, and went out.

Only two more doors. I knocked on the first, waited, knocked again, and went in. A double bed, a table, and an armchair. An open door led to a small bathroom. The blinds were down, the ceiling light was on. In the armchair was Kaminski.

He seemed to be sleeping, his eyes were closed, he was wearing a silk dressing gown several sizes too large for him, with rolled-up sleeves. His hands didn't reach the ends of the arms, the back of it rose high above his head, his feet dangled clear of the floor. His forehead twitched, he turned his head, opened and closed his eyes very quickly, and said, "Who's that?"

"Me," I said. "Zollner. I forgot my bag. Anna had to go to her sister, and asked me if I could stay, no

problem, and . . . I just wanted to let you know. In case you need anything."

"And what would I need?" he said calmly. "Fat cow."

I wondered if I'd heard him right.

"Fat cow," he said again. "And she can't cook either. How much did you pay?"

"I don't know what you mean. But if you have time for a conversation . . ."

"Were you in the cellar?"

"In the cellar?"

He tapped his nose. "You can smell it."

"In which cellar?"

"She knows we can't throw her out. It's impossible to find good help up here."

"Should I . . . switch off the light?"

"The light?" He frowned. "No, no. Pure habit, no."

Maybe he'd taken another pill? I pulled the tape recorder out of my bag, switched it on, and set it on the floor.

"What was that?" he asked.

It would be best to come straight to the point. "Tell me about Matisse!"

He said nothing. I would like to have seen his eyes, but he'd obviously trained himself to keep them shut whenever he wasn't wearing his glasses.

"That house in Nice. I thought: That's how I'd like to live one day. What year are we in?"

"I'm sorry?"

"I know you were in the cellar. What year?"

I told him.

He rubbed his face. I looked at his legs. Two woolly slippers dangled in the air, a hairless, white shin, that of a child, was exposed.

"Where are we?"

"In your house," I said slowly.

"So tell me how much you paid the fat cow!"

"I'll be back later." He drew breath, I left the room quickly and shut the door. It wasn't going to be easy! I would give him a few minutes so that he could collect himself.

I opened the last door and had finally found the office. A desk with a computer, a revolving chair, file cabinets, supplies, piles of paper. I sat down and put my head in my hands. The sun was already low, in the distance the gondola of a funicular climbed the side of a mountain, glittered as it caught a sunbeam, then disappeared over a patch of forest. I could hear crashing and banging from next door; I listened but nothing came of it.

I had to proceed systematically. This was Miriam's workplace, her father probably hadn't been here in years. First I would go through all papers that were

lying open, then I would work my way through the desk drawers from bottom to top, then the cupboards, from left to right. I could be very tidy when I had to.

Most of it was financial records. Bank statements and deposit receipts, involving much less money than I would have thought. Contracts with gallerists: Bogovic had gotten forty percent to begin with, then it came down to thirty, remarkably little, whoever had done the negotiating with him back then had done a good job. Records for private medical insurance—fairly expensive—plus life insurance, for Miriam, oddly enough, but not for that much money. I turned on the computer, it chattered itself into action and asked for the password. I tried *Miriam, Manuel, Adrienne, Papa, Mama, hello,* and *password,* but none of them worked. Crossly, I shut it down again.

Now for the letters: carbon copies of endless correspondence with gallerists about prices, sales, transport of individual paintings, the rights for prints, postcards, illustrated books. Most of the letters were from Miriam, a few had been dictated and signed by her father, only the oldest of them were in his own handwriting: negotiations, proposals, demands, even requests from before he was famous. Back then his handwriting was a scrawl, the lines sloped off to the right, the dots on his *i*'s were all

over the place. Carbon copies of various responses to journalists: *My father is not and never was a representational painter, because he thinks the concept is meaningless, either every painting is representational or none is, and that's all there is to say on the subject.* A few letters from Clure and other friends: arrangements to meet, short replies, birthday greetings, and, in a careful pile, Professor Mehring's Christmas cards. Invitations to lecture at universities; as far as I knew, he never gave lectures, obviously he'd turned them all down. And the photocopy of a curious card to Claes Oldenburg: Kaminski was thanking him for his help, but regretted he had to admit that he thought Oldenburg's art—*Forgive my candor, but in our business friendly lies are the only sin*—was worthless nonsense. Underneath everything else, on the bottom of the last drawer, I found a thick leather portfolio, closed with a little lock. I tried without success to unlock it with the letter opener, then set it aside for later.

I looked at the time: I had to be quick. No letters to Dominik Silva, to Adrienne, to Therese? I heard an engine and took an uneasy look out of the window. A car had stopped downstairs. Clure got out, looked around, took a couple of steps toward Kaminski's house, then turned aside, I let my breath out, and he opened his own garden gate. Next door I could hear Kaminski's dry cough.

I got to the cupboards. I leafed through fat document files, copies of insurance stuff, copies of land registers, he had bought a piece of land in the south of France ten years ago and sold it again at a loss. Copies of trial documents from a court case against a gallerist, who had sold paintings from his early Symbolist period. Also old sketchbooks with detailed drawings of the lines of reflected light between various mirrors: I calculated what they must be worth and struggled for a few seconds against the impulse to pocket one of them. I was on the last cupboard already: old bills, copies of the last eight years' tax returns; I would have loved to go through them, but there wasn't time. Hoping for secret compartments or false bottoms, I tapped the rear walls. I lay down on the floor and peered under the cupboards. Then I got up on the chair and took a look on top of them.

I opened the window, sat on the windowsill, and lit up a cigarette. The wind carried away the ash, and I carefully blew the smoke into the cool air. The sun was already touching one of the peaks, soon it would be gone. So, the last thing left was the portfolio. I flicked the cigarette away, sat down at the desk, and pulled out my pocket knife.

A single smooth incision down the back from top to bottom. The leather was already cracked, and gave way with a crackling sound. I worked the blade care-

fully and slowly. Then opened the portfolio from behind. No one would notice. Why would anyone take it out while Kaminski was still alive? And by then—so what?

There were only a few pages in it. Some lines from Matisse, he wished Kaminski success, had recommended him to several collectors, and assured him of his good wishes and was, his respectfully . . . the next letter was also from Matisse: he was sorry about the failure of the exhibition, but nothing to be done about it, he recommended serious focus and work, work, work, was optimistic about Mr. Kaminski's future, and moreover assured him of his good wishes and . . . a telegram from Picasso: *Walker* wonderful, wish I'd done it, all the best, compadre, live forever! Then, already quite yellowed, three letters in Richard Rieming's small, semi-illegible handwriting. I knew the first, it was reproduced in all Rieming biographies; it was a strange feeling to be holding it in my hand. He was on the ship now, Rieming wrote, and they would never meet again in this life. This was no cause for sorrow, just a fact; and even if after our separation from our mortal bodies there were still ways in which we would endure, it still was not certain that we would remember our old masks and recognize one another again, in other words if there were such a thing as a last farewell,

this was one. His ship was on course for a shore that he still, despite what the books said, and the time-tables, and his own tickets, found unreal. Yet this moment at the end of an existence which had at best been a compromise with what people called Life could not be allowed to pass without serving to ensure that if he, Rieming, had earned the right to call anyone his son, then he would wish to bestow this title on the recipient of this letter. He had led a life barely worthy of the name, had been on earth without knowing why, had carried himself because one must, often freezing, sometimes writing poems, a handful of which had had the luck to find favor. So it did not behoove him to advise someone against following a similar path, and his only wish was that Manuel should be shielded from sorrow, that was already a great deal; indeed it was everything.

Rieming's two other letters were older, written to Kaminski when he was still a schoolboy: in one of them, he advised him not to run away from boarding school again, it didn't help, you had to endure; he didn't want to claim that Manuel would be grateful one day, but he promised him that he would get past it, fundamentally you do get past most things, even when you don't want to. In the other, he announced that *Roadside Words* would be coming out next month, and he was anticipating it with the

anxious joy of a child who feared he was going to get the wrong thing for Christmas, and yet knew that whatever he got, it would also be the right thing. I had no idea what he meant. What all this pointed up was his coldness and affectation. Rieming had always struck me as unpleasant.

The next letter was from Adrienne. She had been thinking about it for a long time, it hadn't been easy for her. She knew it wasn't in Manuel's capacities to make people happy and the word *happy* had a different connotation for him than it did for other people. But she was going to do it, she was going to marry him, she was prepared to take the risk, and if it was a mistake, then she'd make a mistake. This wouldn't come as a surprise to him, but it did come as one to her. She thanked him for giving her time, she was afraid of the future, but perhaps that's the way it had to be, and maybe also she'd be capable one day of saying the words he so longed to hear.

I read it again and wasn't sure what it was that struck me as so weird about it. Now there was only one page left: thin graph paper, like something torn out of an exercise book. I laid it down in front of me and smoothed it flat. It was dated exactly a month before Adrienne's letter. *Manuel, I'm not really writing this. I'm only imagining* . . . an electric buzzing interrupted me: the doorbell.

In a panic I ran downstairs and opened the door. A gray-haired man was leaning on the fence, a felt hat on his head and a fat-bellied bag next to his feet.

"Yes?"

"Doctor Marzeller," he said in a deep voice. "The appointment."

"You have an appointment?"

"He has an appointment. I'm the doctor."

I hadn't expected anything like that. "It's not okay right now," I said, rather choked.

"What isn't okay?"

"Unfortunately it's not okay. Come back tomorrow!"

He took off his hat and stroked his head.

"Mr. Kaminski's working," I said. "He doesn't want to be disturbed."

"You mean he's *painting*?"

"We're working on his biography. He has to concentrate."

"On his biography." He put his hat back on. "Has to concentrate." Why the hell did he have to repeat himself all the time?

"My name is Zollner," I said. "I'm his biographer and friend." I held out my hand, he took it hesitantly. His handshake was uncomfortably strong, I returned it. He looked at me sharply.

"I'm going to him now." He took a step forward.

"No!" I said, blocking him.

He gave me a skeptical glance. Was he wondering if I could stop him? Just try it, I thought.

"Surely it's just routine," I said. "He doesn't need anything."

"And why do you think that?"

"He really is very busy. He can't just interrupt things. There are so many . . . memories. The work means so much to him."

He shrugged his shoulders, blinked, and took a step back. I'd won.

"I'm sorry," I said generously.

"What was your name?" he asked.

"Zollner," I said. "Good-bye."

He nodded. I smiled and he returned my gaze coldly. I closed the door. From the kitchen window I watched as he went to his car, put his bag in the trunk, got behind the wheel, and drove off. Then he stopped, rolled down the window, and looked back at the house again; I jumped back, waited a few seconds, went back to the window, and saw the car heading down the curve. Relieved, I went back upstairs.

Manuel, I'm not really writing this. I'm only imagining that I would write it, but that I wouldn't then stick it in an envelope and send it into the real world, to you. I was just in a cinema, de Gaulle looked as funny as ever in the newsreel, outside it's

thawing, for the first time this year, and I'm trying to imagine that it all has nothing to do with us. When you get right down to it, none of us—not me, not poor Adrienne, not Dominik—believe that they could leave you. But perhaps we're deluding ourselves.

After all this time, I still don't know what we are to you. Maybe we're mirrors (you know all about them) whose task it is to reflect your image and turn you into something large and many-faceted and wide. Yes, you will be famous. And you will have earned it. Now you will go to Adrienne, you'll take what she has to give, and make sure that she believes it will be her own decision when she leaves. Perhaps you'll send her to Dominik. Then there'll be other people, and other mirrors. But not me.

Don't cry, Manuel. You've always cried easily, but this time leave it to me. Naturally it's the end, and we're dying. But that doesn't mean that we won't be here for a long time, that we won't find other people, go for walks, dream at night, and accomplish everything that a marionette can accomplish. I don't know if I'm really writing this, and I don't know if I'll send it. But if I do, if I manage it, and you read it, then please understand that this is what it means: Let me be dead! Don't call, don't come looking for me, because I'm no longer here. And as I look out of the window and ask myself why they all don't . . .

I turned over the page, but there wasn't any more, the rest of it must have gotten lost. I went through all the sheets of paper again, but the missing one wasn't there. Sighing, I pulled out my notepad and wrote the whole thing down. A couple of times my

pencil snapped, my handwriting was so hasty as to be unreadable, but after ten minutes I'd done it. I put all the papers back in the portfolio and put the portfolio all the way at the bottom of the drawer. I closed the cupboards, straightened up the piles of documents, checked that no drawer was still open. I nodded in satisfaction: nobody would notice a thing, I had done it very skillfully. Just at that moment, the sun disappeared, the mountains looked rugged and enormous for a moment, then they retreated and became flat and distant. It was time to play my best card.

I knocked, Kaminski didn't answer.

I went in. He was sitting in his chair, the tape recorder was still lying on the floor. "Back again?" he asked. "Where's Marzeller?"

"The doctor just called. He can't come. Can we talk about Therese Lessing?"

He said nothing.

"Can we talk about Therese Lessing?"

"You must be mad."

"Listen, I'd like . . ."

"What's the matter with Marzeller? Does the guy want me to croak?"

"She's alive, and I've spoken with her."

"Call him. What can he be thinking!"

"I said, she's alive."

"Who?"

"Therese. She's a widow and she's alive. In the north, up on the coast. I have the address."

He didn't reply. He lifted a hand slowly, rubbed his forehead, and let it fall again. His mouth opened and closed, and he frowned. I looked at the tape recorder. The voice-activation function had kicked in, it was recording every word.

"Dominik told you she was dead. But that's wrong."

"It's not true," he said quietly. His chest was rising and falling. I worried about his heart.

"I've known for ten days. It wasn't even hard to discover."

He said nothing. I watched him carefully: he turned his head to the wall, without opening his eyes. His lips were trembling. He puffed his cheeks and blew out the air.

"I'm going to be seeing her soon," I said. "I can ask her anything you want. You just have to tell me what happened back then."

"Who do you think you are?" he whispered.

"Don't you want to know the truth?"

He seemed to be thinking. Now I had him in my hand. That was something he hadn't reckoned with; he too had underestimated Sebastian Zollner! I was so wound up I couldn't stay still, I went to the

window and peered through the slats of the blind. From second to second the lights in the valley were becoming brighter. The bushes stood out round, like copper cutouts, in the twilight.

"I'll be with her next week," I said. "Then I can ask her . . ."

"I don't fly," he said.

"No, of course you don't," I said soothingly. He really was very confused. "You're at home. Everything's fine!"

"The medicines are by the bed."

"That's excellent."

"You imbecile," he said calmly. "You need to pack them."

I gaped at him. "Pack them?"

"We're going to drive."

"You're not serious!"

"Why not?"

"I can pass any questions on to her. We can't do this—no way. You're too—ill." I'd almost said "old." "I can't take the responsibility." Was I dreaming, or were we really having this conversation?

"You're not mistaken, you didn't get something mixed up? Someone didn't pull a fast one on you?"

"Nobody," I said, "would pull a fast one on Sebastian . . ."

He snorted derisively.

"No," I said. "She's alive and"—I hesitated—
"would like to speak to you. You can go to the telephone . . ."

"I'm not going to the telephone. Do you want to
let this opportunity slip?"

I rubbed my forehead. What had happened,
hadn't I just had everything under control? Somehow things had gotten away from me. And he was
right: we'd be driving for two days, I'd never have
been able to hope for so much time with him. I
could ask him whatever I wanted. My book would
become and remain a primary source, read by students and cited by art historians.

"It's strange," he said. "To have you in my life.
Strange and not pleasant."

"You're famous. That's what you wanted. Being
famous means having someone like me." I didn't
know why I said that.

"There's a suitcase in the cupboard. Pack a few of
my things."

I took a deep breath. I couldn't believe it! I had
hoped to surprise and confuse him, in order to get
him to talk about Therese. But I hadn't wanted to
abduct him! "You haven't taken a trip in years."

"The car keys are hanging next to the front door.
You know how to drive, don't you?"

"I'm a very good driver." Did he really intend to

just—right now, just like that, with me? He must be mad. On the other hand: was that my problem? Of course, the journey would endanger his health. But then the book could come out sooner.

"Now what?" he asked.

I sat down on the edge of the bed. Stay calm, I thought, calm! I could just leave it, just walk out; he'd drop off to sleep and by early next morning he'd have forgotten the whole thing. And the opportunity of a lifetime would be over.

"Okay, let's get going!" I cried. I leaped up, the bed creaked, and he winced.

For a few seconds we stayed there frozen, as if he were the one now who couldn't believe it. Then he slowly reached out his hand. I held it, and in that same second I knew that everything was decided. It felt cool and soft, yet its grip was surprisingly strong. I supported him as he slid out of the chair. I stumbled, he pulled me to the door. In the passage he stopped, I gave him a firm push. On the stairs I wouldn't have been able to say anymore which of us was leading the other.

"Not so fast," I said hoarsely. "I still have to get your luggage."

VII

So now I really was driving the BMW. The road dropped away steeply behind us, the headlights only pulled in a few yards of asphalt out of the darkness; it was hard navigating the bends. Another one: I hauled on the steering wheel, the road curved and kept curving, I thought that might be it now, but no, it kept on curving, we came dangerously near to the right edge, the engine coughed, I changed down, the engine howled, and the curve was behind us.

"You need to change gears earlier," said Kaminski.

I bit off any reply, the next curve was already coming up and I had to concentrate: shift, easy on the gas, shift down, the engine gave a deep rumble, the road stretched straight ahead of us.

"You see!" he said.

I heard his lips smack, saw his jaw working out of

the corner of my eye. He had put on his dark glasses, folded his hands in his lap, and leaned back. Over his shirt and pullover he was still wearing the dressing gown. I had tied his shoelaces and fastened him into his seatbelt, but he immediately undid the buckle again. He looked pale and agitated. I opened the glove compartment and put the tape recorder in it.

"When was the last time you met Rieming?"

"The day before his ship sailed. We went for a walk, he was wearing two coats, one on top of the other, because he was cold. I said I was having problems seeing, he said, 'Use your memory!' He kept clapping his hands, and his eyes were watering. Chronic inflammation. He was very worried about the journey, water terrified him. Richard was afraid of everything."

Suddenly we were heading into the longest curve I'd ever seen: it felt as if we were turning in a full circle for almost a minute. "And his relationship with your mother?"

He said nothing. The houses of the village suddenly appeared: black shadows, lighted windows, the name of the place on a road sign, for a few seconds streetlights swayed above us, the main square was lit up with its shop displays, then another road sign, this time with a line through the place name, then darkness again.

"He was simply there. He was given something to eat, he read his newspaper, and in the evenings he went to his room to work. Mama and he always used the formal 'Sie' when they spoke to each other."

The curves were less tight now. I eased my grip on the steering wheel and sat back. I was gradually getting used to it.

"Naturally he had no desire to have my scribblings in his book, but he was afraid of me."

"Really?"

Kaminski sniggered. "I was fifteen and a little crazy. Poor Richard thought I was capable of anything. A pleasant child I most certainly was not!"

I kept quiet because I was annoyed. Of course, what he'd just told me would be a sensation, but he was probably just trying to trick me, it just didn't sound plausible. Who could I check with? The man sitting beside me was the last person alive who had known Rieming. And everything that Rieming had been, outside his books—the two coats, the hand-clapping, the fear, and the watering eyes—would disappear along with his memory. And perhaps I for once would be the only one who could still recall . . . what was the matter with me?

"With Matisse it was the same thing. He wanted to throw me out. But I wouldn't go. He didn't like my paintings. But I wouldn't go! You know how it is

when somebody simply won't go? You can achieve a lot that way."

"I know. When I was writing my account of the Wernicke thing . . ."

"So what could he do? He finally sent me to a collector."

"To Dominik Silva."

"Oh, he was so great and so reserved and impressive, and I couldn't have cared less. A young artist is a strange creature. Half crazed with ambition and greed."

A last curve opened out onto the main road. The mushroom-shaped roof of the railroad station shot into view, the valley was so narrow that the tracks ran right next to the road. An oncoming car stopped and honked its horn, I drove past regardless, and only then noticed that I was still driving with my brights. Another car braked sharply and I dropped my lights to normal. I avoided the entrance to the highway, I really didn't want to have to pay tolls. The roads in any case were empty at this hour. Shadows of forests, a village without lights, it was like driving through a dead land. I opened the window a crack, feeling almost weightless and unreal. Night, in a car, alone with the greatest painter in the world. Who could have imagined it a week ago?

"May I smoke?"

He didn't answer, he was asleep. I coughed as loudly as I could, but it didn't help, he didn't wake up. I hummed to myself. He was supposed to be talking to me! I finally gave up and switched off the tape recorder. For a while I listened to him snore, then I lit a cigarette. But not even the smoke woke him. So why did he need sleeping pills?

I blinked, suddenly I felt as though I'd nodded off. I jerked back again, upright, but nothing had happened, Kaminski snored on, the road was empty, and I steered back into the right lane. An hour later he surfaced and told me to stop because he needed to get out. I was worried and asked if he needed my help; he muttered that that would make his day, climbed out of the car, and fumbled at his pants in the cone of the headlights. Groping for the car roof, he then eased himself back into his seat and closed the door. I drove on and a few seconds later he was snoring again. Once he murmured in his sleep, his head lolled this way and that, and he gave off a faint old man's smell.

Dawn slowly brought the mountains into the foreground as the sky receded, and across the plain in scattered houses, lights began to switch themselves on and off. The sun came up and climbed higher in the sky, I pulled down the visor. The road soon filled up with cars, trucks, and one tractor after

another, which I overtook with my hand on the horn. Kaminski sighed.

"Is there any coffee?" he asked suddenly.

"It can be arranged."

He cleared his throat, blew through his nose, moved his lips, and cocked an ear in my direction. "Who are you?"

My heart skipped a beat. "Zollner!"

"Where are we going?"

"To . . ." I swallowed. "To Therese, your . . . to Therese Lessing. We had . . . you had—this idea yesterday. I wanted to help."

He seemed to be thinking. He wrinkled his brow and his head trembled a little.

"Should we go back?" I asked.

He shrugged, took off his glasses, folded them, and stuck them in the breast pocket of his dressing gown. His eyes were closed. He ran his fingers over his teeth.

"Do I get breakfast?"

"We can stop at the next rest area . . ."

"Breakfast!" he said again, and spat. Just like that, on the floor in front of him. I stared at him, shocked. He lifted his big hands and rubbed his eyes.

"Zollner," he said hoarsely, "yes?"

"Correct."

"Do you paint yourself?"

"Not anymore. I tried, but when I failed the entrance exam for art college, I gave up. Maybe a mistake! I should start again."

"No."

"I did color compositions in the style of Yves Klein. There were people who liked them. But it would be really dumb; if I just went at it seriously . . ."

"That's what I mean." He put his glasses ceremoniously back on his nose. "Breakfast!"

I lit yet another cigarette, it didn't seem to disturb him. Which, for a moment, I regretted. I blew the smoke in his direction. A sign pointed to a rest area, I drove into the parking lot, got out, and shut the door behind me.

I deliberately took my time, he could just damn well wait. The restaurant was dusty and full of stale smoke, there were hardly any customers. I ordered two cups of coffee and five croissants. "Pack them properly, coffee not too weak!" Nobody had ever complained about her coffee, said the sluglike waitress. I said she must be mistaking me for someone who cared. She asked if I was looking for trouble. I said she should get moving.

Balancing them carefully, I made it back to the car with the steaming cups and the paper bag full of croissants. The rear door was open, and there was a

man on the backseat talking to Kaminski. He was thin, with horn-rimmed glasses, greasy hair, and protruding teeth, and next to him on the seat was a backpack. "Think, dear sir," he was saying. "Prudence is everything. Evil disguises itself as the easier path." Kaminski smiled and nodded. I got behind the steering wheel, slammed the door shut, looked inquiringly from one to the other.

"This is Karl Ludwig," said Kaminski in a way that implied any further question was superfluous.

"Call me Karl Ludwig."

"He's coming with us for the next bit," said Kaminski.

"We don't take hitchhikers!"

There was silence for a few seconds. Karl Ludwig sighed. "I told you so, dear sir."

"Rubbish," said Kaminski. "Zollner, if I'm not mistaken, this is my car."

"Yes, but . . ."

"Give me the coffee and drive!"

I held out the coffee, a little too high on purpose, he groped for it, found it, and took it. I put the paper bag in his lap, drank all my coffee, it was too weak of course, threw the cup out the window, and turned the key in the ignition. The parking lot and the rest area shrank in the rearview mirror.

"May I ask where you're going?" asked Karl Ludwig.

"Of course," said Kaminski.

"Where are you going?"

"It's personal," I said.

"I'm sure it is, but . . ."

"What I mean is, it's none of your business."

"You're quite right." Karl Ludwig nodded. "Excuse me, Mr. Zollner."

"How did you get my name?"

"Dear God," said Kaminski, "because I just used it."

"That's exactly right," said Karl Ludwig.

"Tell us about yourself!" said Kaminski.

"There's not much to tell. I've had a hard life."

"Who hasn't?" said Kaminski.

"Truly spoken, dear sir!"

Karl Ludwig tugged at his glasses. "You see, I was someone once. Piercing glance the world to muster, heart that feels each heart's desire, passion's glow for women's luster, voice that sings, my own, my fire. And now? Look at me!"

I lit a cigarette. "What was that with the women?"

"That was Goethe," said Kaminski. "Don't you know anything? Give me one too."

"You're not allowed to smoke."

"Right," said Kaminski, stretching out his hand.

I realized that all things considered, it was in my interest, and gave it to him. For a few seconds I could feel Karl Ludwig's eyes on me in the rearview mirror. I sighed and held the packet over my head so that he could take one. He reached out, I felt his soft, clammy fingers close over mine and pull the packet out of my hand.

"Hey!" I yelled.

"You two, if I may say so, strike me as really odd."

"What do you mean?"

His eyes in the mirror again: narrow, focused, malicious. He showed his teeth. "You're not related, you're not teacher and pupil, and you don't work together. And he"—he lifted a skinny finger and pointed at Kaminski—"seems familiar to me. You don't."

"There are reasons for that," said Kaminski.

"So I would guess!" said Karl Ludwig. The two of them laughed. What was going on here?

"Give me back the cigarettes," I said.

"How careless of me. Please forgive me." Karl Ludwig didn't move. I rubbed my eyes; suddenly I felt weak.

"Dear sir," said Karl Ludwig. "The majority of life is falsehood and waste. We encounter evil and we know it not. Would you like to hear more?"

"No," I said.

"Yes," said Kaminski. "Do you know Hieronymus Bosch?"

Karl Ludwig nodded. "He painted the devil."

"That's not confirmed." Kaminski sat up. "You mean the figure with the chamber pot on its head, eating people, in the far right in *The Garden of Earthly Delights*."

"Further up," said Karl Ludwig. "The man growing out of a tree."

"Interesting idea," said Kaminski, "the only figure that's looking out of the picture and showing its pain. But you're on the wrong track."

Furious, I looked from one to the other. What were they talking about?

"That's not the devil!" said Kaminski. "It's a self-portrait."

"Is there a contradiction?" asked Karl Ludwig.

There was silence for a few moments. In the rearview mirror, Karl Ludwig was smiling. Kaminski, nonplussed, chewed his lower lip.

"I think you took the wrong exit," said Karl Ludwig.

"You don't even know where we're going," I said.

"So where are you going?"

"Not bad," said Kaminski, reaching back to pass him the croissants. "The tree man. Not bad!" Karl Ludwig tore the paper and began to eat greedily.

"You were saying you had a hard life," said Kaminski. "I can still remember my first exhibition. What a catastrophe."

"I've exhibited too," said Karl Ludwig through a mouthful.

"Really?"

"Privately. A long time ago."

"Paintings?"

"Something of that sort."

"I bet you were good," said Kaminski.

"I don't think one could say that."

"Was it tough for you?" I asked.

"Well, yes," said Karl Ludwig. "In principle, anyway. I had . . ."

"I wasn't asking you!" A sports car was driving too slow, I honked and overtook it.

"It was okay," said Kaminski. "By chance I didn't have any worries about money."

"Thanks to Dominik Silva."

"And I had enough ideas. I knew my time would come. Ambition is like a childhood illness. You get over it and it strengthens you."

"Some people don't," said Karl Ludwig.

"And besides, Therese Lessing was still there," I said.

Kaminski didn't answer. I gave him a sharp side-

ways look: his expression had darkened. In the rear-view mirror Karl Ludwig was wiping his mouth with his hand. Crumbs trickled down onto the leather upholstery.

"I want to go home," said Kaminski.

"Excuse me!"

"Nothing to excuse. Take me home!"

"Perhaps we should talk about it in peace and quiet."

He turned his head, and for a long moment the feeling that he was looking at me through his dark glasses was so strong that it took my breath away. Then he turned away, his head sank down onto his chest, and his whole body seemed to shrivel.

"Fine," I said quietly, "we'll go back." Karl Ludwig sniggered. I signaled, pulled off the road, and turned around.

"On," said Kaminski.

"What?"

"We're going on."

"But you just said . . ."

He hissed, and I shut up. His face was hard, as if chiseled. Had he really changed his mind, or was he simply demonstrating his power to me? No, he was old and confused, I shouldn't overestimate him. I turned around again and drove back onto the road.

"Sometimes it's hard to decide," said Karl Ludwig.

"Be quiet," I said. Kaminski's jaws were chewing on nothing, his face had gone slack again, as if nothing had happened.

"Besides," I said, "I was in Clairance."

"Where?"

"In the salt mine."

"You're certainly making an effort!" Kaminski said loudly.

"Did you really get lost in there?"

"I know it sounds ridiculous. I couldn't find the guide again. Until then, I hadn't taken the thing with my eyes seriously. But suddenly there was a mist everywhere. And there couldn't be any mist down there. So I had a problem."

"Macular degeneration?" asked Karl Ludwig.

"What?" I asked.

Kaminski nodded. "Good guess."

"Do you make out anything at all these days?" asked Karl Ludwig.

"Shapes, sometimes colors. Outlines, if I'm lucky."

"Did you find your way out by yourself?" I asked.

"Yes, thank God. I used the old trick: keep following the right-hand wall."

"I understand." The right-hand wall? I tried to picture it. Why should that work?

"Next day I went to the eye doctor. That's when I found out."

"You must have thought the world was going under," said Karl Ludwig.

Kaminski nodded slowly. "And you know what?"

Karl Ludwig leaned forward.

"It went under."

The sun was almost at its zenith, the mountains, already far behind us, shimmered in the midday heat. I had to yawn, a pleasant exhaustion crept over me. I began to talk about my Wernicke book. How I had heard about the incident by chance, luck is often the father of great achievements, and I was the first to get to the house and had peered through the window. I described the widow's fruitless attempts to get rid of me. As always, the story was well received: Kaminski smiled pensively, Karl Ludwig looked at me open-mouthed. I stopped at the next gas station.

While I filled the tank, Kaminski got out. Groaning, he smoothed down his dressing gown, pressed one hand against his back, pulled the cane into position, and straightened up. "Take me to the toilet!"

I nodded. "Karl Ludwig, out!"

Karl Ludwig took his time putting on his glasses and bared his teeth. "Why?"

"I'm locking the car."

"No problem, I'll stay in it."

"That's why."

"Do you want to insult him?" asked Kaminski.

"You're insulting me," said Karl Ludwig.

"He hasn't done anything to you!"

"I haven't done anything!"

"So stop that nonsense!"

"Yes, please—I beg you!"

I sighed, bent down, put the tape recorder away, pulled out the car key, gave Karl Ludwig a warning glance, shouldered my bag, and reached for Kaminski's hand. Again his soft, oddly certain touch, again the feeling that he was the one leading me. As I waited, I looked at advertising posters: Drink Beer!, a laughing housewife, three fat children, a round teapot with a laughing face. I leaned my head against the wall for a moment; I really was very tired.

We went to the cashier. "I don't have any money with me," said Kaminski.

I bit my teeth and pulled out my credit card. Outside an engine started up, died, started up again, and then receded into the distance; the woman at the cash register looked up curiously at the surveillance monitor. I signed, and took Kaminski by the arm. The door hissed as it opened.

I stopped so abruptly that Kaminski almost fell.

And yet: I really wasn't surprised. I felt it was

inevitable, that some essential piece of a composition had fallen into place. I wasn't even shocked. I rubbed my eyes. I wanted to scream, but I didn't have the strength. I sank slowly to my knees, sat down on the ground, and propped my head in my hands.

"Now what?" said Kaminski.

I closed my eyes. Suddenly, I just didn't care. He, and my book, and my future could all go to hell! What concern of mine was all this, what did this old man have to do with me? The asphalt was warm, the dark streaked with light, it smelled of grass and gasoline.

"Zollner, are you dead?"

I opened my eyes and stood up slowly.

"Zollner!" roared Kaminski. His voice was high and cut like a knife. I left him standing there and went back in. The woman at the cash register was laughing as if she'd never seen anything so funny. "Zollner!" She picked up the phone receiver, I stopped her, the police would just hold us up and ask inconvenient questions. I said I would take care of things myself. "Zollner!" She should simply call us a taxi. She did so, then she wanted money for the phone call. I asked her if she was mad, went out, and took Kaminski by the elbow.

"So there you are. What's wrong?"

"Don't behave as if you don't know."

I looked around. A light wind was making waves run across the fields, a few thin clouds hung in the sky. Basically it was a peaceful place. We could stay here.

But our taxi was arriving already. I helped Kaminski into the backseat and asked the driver to take us to the nearest railroad station.

VIII

THE RINGING OF A TELEPHONE jolted me out of sleep. I groped for the receiver, something fell to the ground. I found it and pulled it toward me. Who? Wegenfeld, Anselm Wegenfeld, from reception. Fine, I said, what is it? The room I found myself looking at was a shabby hodgepodge: bedposts, table, a stained bedside lamp, a mirror hung squint. The old gentleman, said Wegenfeld. Who? The old gentleman, he repeated with peculiar emphasis. I sat up, wide awake. "What's happened?"

"Nothing, but you should check in on him."

"Why?"

Wegenfeld cleared his throat, coughed, cleared his throat again. "There are rules in this house. You'll understand that there are some things we just cannot tolerate. You understand?"

"Dammit, what's going on?"

"Let's say, he has a visitor. Either you get rid of her, or we will!"

"You're not trying to say . . . ?"

"Yes I am," said Wegenfeld. "That's exactly what I'm trying to say."

I stood up, went into the tiny bathroom, and washed my face with cold water. It was five in the afternoon, I had been so deep asleep I'd lost all sense of time. It took a moment or two for my memory to start functioning.

A silent taxi driver had collected us at the gas station. "No," Kaminski said suddenly. "Not to the station. I want to lie down."

"You can't right now."

"I can and I will. Drive to a hotel!"

The driver nodded phlegmatically.

"It'll only hold us up," I said. "We have to get on." The driver shrugged.

"It's just turned one o'clock," said Kaminski.

I looked at the time, it was twelve fifty-five. "Nowhere near it."

"At one o'clock I lie down. I've been doing it for forty years and I'm not going to change. I can also ask this gentleman to drive me home."

The driver threw him a greedy look.

"Well, all right," I said, "to a hotel." I felt empty

and helpless. I tapped the driver on the shoulder. "The best in the neighborhood." As I said the word "best," I shook my head and flapped my hand. He understood and grinned.

"I don't use the other kind either," said Kaminski.

I slipped the driver a twenty. He winked. "I'm taking you to the very best!"

"I hope so," said Kaminski, pulled his dressing gown tighter, held tight to his stick, and smacked his lips quietly. It didn't seem to bother him at all that his car and luggage were gone, along with my suitcase and my new shaver; all I had left was my bag. He simply hadn't taken in what had happened. Probably it was better not to talk about it.

A small town: low houses, shop windows, a pedestrian precinct with the usual fountain, more shop windows, a large hotel and a larger one, both of which we drove past. We stopped in front of a small, shabby boardinghouse. I looked at the driver, cocked an eyebrow, and rubbed my thumb against my forefinger. Was this really the cheapest? He thought for a moment and then drove on.

We stopped in front of an even more wretched-looking hotel with a dirt-encrusted façade and filthy windows. I nodded. "Great! Do you see that man in livery!"

"Two of them," said the taxi driver, who was

obviously enjoying himself. "When government ministers come, they always stay here."

I paid, gave him another tip, he'd earned it, and led Kaminski into the small, dirty lobby. A depressing stopover for commercial travelers. "What a carpet!" I said admiringly and demanded two rooms. A man with greasy hair looked surprised and handed me the registration book. On the left-hand page I wrote my name, on the right I scribbled something illegible. "Thank you, no porters?" I said loudly and led Kaminski to the elevator; the car rose groaningly and delivered us to a corridor that was barely lit. His room was tiny, the cupboard gaped open, and the air was stale.

"There's a genuine Chagall hanging there!" I said.

"There are more of Marc's originals than there are copies. Put the medicines next to the bed. It smells strange, are you sure this is a good hotel?"

The bedside table barely provided enough space for them all; luckily I'd packed everything in my bag yesterday: beta-blockers, cardio-aspirin, blood thinner, sleeping pills.

"Where's my suitcase?" he asked.

"Your suitcase is in the car."

He frowned. "The tree man," he said. "Remarkable! Have you ever focused on Bosch?"

"Not really."

"Then off you go!" He clapped his hands merrily. "Go!"

"If you need anything . . ."

"I don't need a thing, now go!"

I sighed and left. In my room, which was even tinier than his, I undressed, got into bed naked, hid my head under the coverlet, and dozed off. When Wegenfeld called, I had been dead to the world for three hours.

It took me some time to find Kaminski's room again. There was a DO NOT DISTURB sign on the door, but the door wasn't closed. I opened it quietly.

". . . he had this idea," Kaminski was saying, "to keep painting himself, with this mixture of hate and self-love. He was the only megalomaniac who was absolutely right." The woman was sitting on the bed, bolt upright, legs crossed, back against the wall. She was heavily made up, with red hair, a see-through blouse, a short skirt, and fishnet stockings. Her boots were set neatly side by side on the floor. Kaminski, fully dressed and in his dressing gown, was lying on his back, hands folded on his chest, his head on her lap. "So I asked him: Does it have to be the Mino-taur? We were in his extremely orderly studio, he only ever messed it up when photos were going to be taken, and he looked at me with those black eyes of his, a god's eyes." The woman yawned and slowly

stroked his head. "I said, the Minotaur—don't you think you're taking yourself a little too seriously? And he never forgave me. If I'd laughed at his pictures, he wouldn't have cared less. Come in, Zollner!"

I closed the door behind me.

"Have you noticed how she smells? No expensive perfume, and a bit too strong, but what an effect! What's your name?"

She looked at me for a moment. "Jana."

"Sebastian, be glad you're young!"

He had never used my first name before. I inhaled the air to test it, but there was no hint of perfume. "This really isn't okay," I said. "She was noticed on her way in. The manager called."

"Tell him who I am!"

Disconcerted, I said nothing. On the table was a small notepad, with only a few sheets on it, left behind by some previous guest. There was a drawing on it. Kaminski maneuvered himself laboriously into a sitting position. "Just a joke. You're going to have to go now, Jana. I'm very grateful to you."

"That's fine," she said, and began to put on her boots. I watched attentively as the leather stretched itself over her knee, for a moment her collarbone was exposed, her red hair slid down softly over the nape of her neck. I snatched the notepad, tore off the

top sheet, and pocketed it. I opened the door, Jana followed me out silently.

"Don't worry," she said, "he's paid already."

"Really?" And before, he'd insisted he had no money with him! But I couldn't let an opportunity like this slip. "Come with me!" I led her into my room, shut the door behind her, and gave her a twenty. "There's something I want to know."

She leaned against the wall and looked at me. She must have been nineteen or twenty, no older than that. She crossed her arms, lifted one foot, and ground the sole of her boot into the carpet, it was going to leave the most awful mark, then she took a look at my ravaged bed and smiled. To my annoyance, I could feel myself blushing.

"Jana . . ." I cleared my throat. "May I call you Jana?" I had to be careful not to unsettle her.

She shrugged.

"Jana, what did he want?"

"What?"

"What does he like?"

She frowned.

"What did you have to do?"

She took a step to one side, away from me. "You saw."

"And before that? That wasn't all . . ."

"Of course it was!" She looked at me in disbelief. "You can see how old he is. What's your problem?"

He must have imagined the perfume. I pulled up the only chair, sat down, felt insecure, stood up again. "All he did was talk? And you stroked his head?"

She nodded.

"Don't you think that's weird?"

"Not really."

"Where did he get your phone number?"

"From Information, I think. He's pretty sharp." She pushed back her hair. "So who is he? There must have been a time when he . . . !" She smiled. "Well, you know. He's not related to you, is he?"

"Why do you say that?" I remembered that Karl Ludwig had said the same thing. "I mean, why not, why do you think that?"

"Oh, it's obvious! Can I go now . . ." She looked me in the eyes. ". . . or is there something you still want?"

I went hot all over. "Why would you think we're not related?"

She looked at me for a few moments, then she came toward me, and I involuntarily took a step back. She reached out her arms, ran both hands over my head, took hold of me by the neck, and pulled me to her. I pulled away, I saw her eyes up close to

mine, and didn't know where to look, her hair was in my face, I tried to get loose, she laughed and stepped back, suddenly I felt crippled.

"I've been paid," she said. "Now what?"

I didn't reply.

"You see?" she said, raising her eyebrows. "Don't make a big thing of it!" She laughed and went out.

I rubbed my forehead. After a while my breathing went back to normal. Well, great! Once again I'd thrown money out the window; it couldn't go on this way! I had to talk to Megelbach about expenses as soon as possible.

I pulled out the sheet of paper I'd torn off the notebook. A web of straight—no, very slightly angled lines that spread out over the paper from the two bottom corners in a fine network of spaces that generated the outlines of a human figure. Or did it? Now I couldn't see it anymore. Yes, there it was again! And then it was gone again. The pencil strokes were confident, unhesitating, each running from its starting point without a break. Could a blind man do this? Or had it been someone else, a previous guest, and the whole thing was an accident? I would have to show it to Komenev, I couldn't clarify it on my own. I folded up the sheet of paper, stuck it back in my pocket, and asked myself why I'd let her go. I called Megelbach.

Nice to talk to you, he said, and how was I getting on? Terrific, I said, better than expected, the old man had already said things to me I could never have hoped for, I could promise him a sensation, but I wasn't going to give away anything more right now. It was just that I had unexpected expenses and . . . a hissing noise interrupted me. Expenses, I said again, that . . . the connection was terrible, said Megelbach, could I call back later? But it was important, I said, I urgently needed . . . not a good moment, said Megelbach, he was in the middle of a meeting and didn't know why his secretary had put me through at all. It was only a small thing, I said, a . . . good luck! he cried, good luck, he was sure we were on to something great. Then he hung up. I called back, this time the secretary answered. She was sorry, but Mr. Megelbach was not in the office. No, no, I said, I had just been . . . did I wish, she said cattily, to leave a message? I said I would try again later.

I went to Kaminski. A sweating waiter with a tray was just knocking at his door.

"What's this supposed to be?" I asked. "Nobody ordered this!"

The waiter licked his lips and scowled at me. Sweat was pearling on his forehead. "Yes they did. Room three-oh-four. Just called. Daily special, double

portion. We don't actually have room service, but he said he'd pay extra."

"Finally!" Kaminski yelled from inside. "Bring it in, you'll have to cut up the meat for me! Not now, Zollner!"

I turned around and went back to my room.

As I came in, the telephone was ringing. Probably Megelbach, wanting to apologize. I grabbed the receiver, but all I could hear was the dial tone. I had the wrong instrument, it was my cell phone.

"Where are you?" screamed Miriam. "Is he with you?"

I pressed the disconnect button.

The phone rang again. I picked it up, set it aside, and thought. Then I took a deep breath and answered.

"Hello!" I said. "How are you? And how did you get this number? I promise you . . ."

I didn't get to say any more. I walked slowly up and down, went to the window, leaned my forehead against the glass. I lowered the phone and breathed out: a fine mist spread over the pane. I put the thing back to my ear.

"Don't be ridiculous," I said, "abduction? He's in great shape, we're just taking a trip together. You can join us if you'd like."

I had to yank the telephone away, my ear hurt. I

rubbed my sleeve over the hazy window. Although I was holding the contraption almost two feet away from my head, I could understand every word.

"Can I say something too?"

I sat down on the bed. With my free hand I turned on the TV. A rider was galloping through a gulch in the desert; I changed channels, a housewife was gazing passionately at a hand towel, I changed channels, a female talking head was pontificating into a microphone, I switched it off.

"Can I say something too?"

This time it worked. She fell silent so suddenly that I was unprepared for it. For a few seconds we both were listening, startled, to each other's silence.

"First, I am not even going to respond to the word *abduction*, I will not sink to such a level. Your father asked me to accompany him. I had to change all my other appointments, but out of my deepest admiration and . . . friendship, I did it for him. I have our conversation about it on tape. So forget about the police, you'd just be making a fool of yourself. We're in a first-class hotel, your father's gone back to his room and doesn't want to be disturbed, I'll be bringing him back tomorrow evening. Second, I haven't been rummaging through anything! Not your cellar and not any desk either. That's a disgusting insinuation!" Now she must be

realizing she'd picked the wrong person to go after.
"And fourth . . ." I faltered. "Third, I'm not giving
you any information about where we're going. He
can tell you that himself. I feel very . . . beholden to
him." I stood up, pleased with the way my voice
sounded. "He's visibly blossoming! Freedom does
him good! If I told you what he just . . . it was high
time somebody got him out of that prison."

What? I listened in amazement. Had I misheard? I
bent forward and put the phone to my other ear. No,
I hadn't.

"Do you find that funny?"

I was in such a rage I banged my knee on the bedside table. "Yes, that's what I said. Out of that
prison." I went to the window. The sun was low
behind roofs, turrets, and antennae. "Prison! If you
don't stop laughing I'm going to hang up. Do you
hear? If you don't . . ."

I hit the disconnect button.

Throwing the phone away, I started pacing, so
angry I could hardly breathe. I rubbed my knee. It
wasn't smart to have simply broken off the conversation like that. I thumped the table, bent over, and
gradually felt my rage drain away. I waited. But to my
surprise, she didn't call back.

Actually, it had gone well. She didn't take me seriously, so she wouldn't take any drastic measures. No

matter what she'd found funny, I'd obviously said the right thing. Once again, I just had this gift for it.

I looked in the mirror. Perhaps he'd been right. No bald spot, of course, but a barely perceptibly receding hairline, that made my face look rounder, older, and a little paler. I wasn't so young anymore. I stood up. My jacket didn't hang well, either. I raised my hand and let it drop again, my mirror image tentatively did the same. Or wasn't it the fault of the jacket? There was something off-balance in the way I held myself, that I'd never noticed before. *Don't make a big thing of it!* Of what, for God's sake? *Maybe you still have a chance.*

No, I had spent too much time behind the steering wheel, I was simply overtired. What were they all implying? I shook my head, looked at myself in the mirror, then hastily looked away again. What in the world were they all implying?

IX

"PERSPECTIVE IS A TECHNIQUE of abstraction, a convention of the Quattrocento that we have accustomed ourselves to. Light has to pass through many lenses before we consider a picture to be realistic. Reality has never looked anything like a photograph."

"No?" I said, suppressing a yawn. We were sitting in the dining car of an express train. Kaminski was wearing his glasses, his stick was propped beside him, and the dressing gown was rolled up in a plastic bag in the luggage rack. The tape recorder was switched on, and lying on the table. He had eaten soup, two main courses, and a dessert, and was now on his coffee; I had cut up his meat for him and made a futile attempt to remind him of his diet. He

was in an expansive mood and full of good cheer; he'd been talking for two hours straight.

"Reality changes with every glance, at every second. Perspective is an assemblage of rules that tries to trap all this chaos onto one flat surface. No more, no less."

"Oh yes?" I was hungry: in contrast to him, all I'd eaten was an inedible salad, dry leaves in a greasy dressing, and when I'd complained, all the waiter did was sigh. The recorder clicked, the end of another tape, I put a new one in. He had really succeeded this whole time in saying absolutely nothing that was usable.

"Truth is to be found, if anywhere, in atmosphere. That's to say, in color rather than in drawing, and absolutely never in deep perspective. Did your professor never tell you that?"

"No, no." I hadn't the foggiest idea. My memories of university were hazy at best: pointless discussions in seminar rooms, pale fellow students who were terrified of the lecturers, the smell of stale food in the cafeteria, and someone always asking you to sign a petition. Once I'd had to deliver an essay on Degas. Degas? I couldn't think of a single thing to say, so I copied it all out of the encyclopedia. After two semesters I got the job at the advertising agency, thanks to my uncle, shortly after that the job of art

critic on the local newspaper came free, and my application was successful. I got things right from the start: some beginners tried to make a name for themselves by writing savage takedowns, but that wasn't the way things worked. It was much better always and in everything to have exactly the same opinions as your colleagues and attend all the openings to network. It wasn't long before I was writing for several magazines, which allowed me to give up my job.

"Nobody has ever drawn better than Michelangelo, nobody could draw like him. But color didn't mean much to him. Look at the Sistine Chapel: it really wasn't clear to him that colors . . . tell us something about the world too. Are you taping this?"

"Every word."

"You know that I experimented with the techniques of the Old Masters. There was a period when I even prepared all my own colors. I learned to distinguish pigments by their smell. If you practice, you can even mix them without making a mistake. So I could see better than my assistant with his two sharp eyes."

Two men sat down at the next table. "It comes down to the four Ps," said one of them. "Price, Promotion, Positioning, Product."

"Look out the window!" said Kaminski. He leaned back and rubbed his forehead; again I was struck by how large his hands were. The skin was cracked, there were scarred welts around his knuckles: the hands of a laborer. "I take it there are hills and meadows and the occasional village. Am I right?"

I smiled. "More or less."

"Is the sun shining?"

"Yes." It was raining cats and dogs. And for the last half hour I had seen nothing but crowded streets, warehouses, and factory chimneys. No hills or meadows, and not a village to be had.

"I wondered once whether one could paint a train journey. The whole journey, not just a single snapshot."

"Our focus groups," said the man at the next table loudly, "report that the texture has improved, as has the taste!" I took the precaution of pushing the tape recorder closer to Kaminski. If the guy over there didn't quiet down, he'd be the only thing you could hear on the tape.

"I often thought about it," said Kaminski, "after I had to stop. How does a painting deal with time? Back then I was thinking about the journey between Paris and Lyon. You'd have to paint it the way you see it in your memory—*compressed*."

"We haven't talked about your marriage yet, Manuel."

He frowned.

"We haven't . . ." I tried again.

"Please do not address me by my first name. I am older than you are and I am accustomed to different manners."

"The million-dollar question," brayed the man at the next table, "is, will the European markets react differently?"

I turned around. He was in his early thirties, and his jacket hung badly. He was pale and his sparse hair was combed over his head. Exactly the kind of person I couldn't stand.

"The million-dollar question!" he brayed again, and then saw me looking at him. "What?"

"Keep your voice down," I said.

"I am keeping it down!"

"Then try a little further down!" I turned back again.

"It would have to be a large canvas," Kaminski was saying, "and although nothing seems to be clear, everyone who's ever made that trip should be able to recognize it. Back then, I thought I could pull it off."

"And then there's the question of location,"

brayed the man at the next table. "I ask, what are the priorities? And they have no idea!"

I turned around and looked at him.

"Are you looking at me?" he asked.

"No!" I said.

"Arrogant bastard!"

"Clown!"

"I won't take that," he said and stood up.

"Maybe you'll have to." I got to my feet too, and realized that he was a lot bigger than I was. Conversation in the carriage stopped.

"Sit down," said Kaminski in a voice I didn't recognize.

The man, suddenly unsure of himself, stepped forward and then back again. He looked at the other man at his table, then at Kaminski. He fingered his brow. Then he sat down.

"Very good!" I said. "That was . . ."

"You too!"

I sat down at once. I stared at him, my heart thumping.

He leaned back, stroking the coffee cup. "It's exactly one o'clock and I have to lie down."

"I know." I closed my eyes for a moment. What had frightened me so much? "We'll be at the apartment very soon."

"I want a hotel."

Then pay for one, I wanted to say, but managed not to. This morning I'd had to pick up the hotel charges again, along with his room service. While I was giving Mr. Wegenfeld my credit card, I remembered Kaminski's bank statement. This mean little old man who was traveling, sleeping, and eating at my expense still had more money than I would ever earn.

"We're staying privately, with a . . . with me. A large apartment, very comfortable. You'll like it."

"I want a hotel."

"You'll like it!" Elke wouldn't be back till tomorrow afternoon, we'd be gone by then, she probably wouldn't even notice. Pacified, I noticed that the ape at the next table was now talking quietly. I'd really put the fear of God into him.

"Give me a cigarette!" said Kaminski.

"You're not supposed to smoke."

"Whatever speeds things up is fine by me. You too, no? Painting, I wanted to say, is all about problem solving, just like in science." I gave him a cigarette and he lit it with a trembling hand. What had he said—me too? Had he guessed something?

"For example, I wanted to do a series of self-portraits, but not using my reflection in a mirror or

photos, just drawing on the image I had of myself. Nobody has any idea what they really look like, we have completely false pictures of ourselves. Normally you try to even things out, using whatever you can. But if you do the opposite, if you intentionally paint this false picture, as accurately as possible, in every detail, with every characteristic trait . . . !" He banged on the table. "A portrait that isn't a portrait! Can you imagine such a thing? But nothing came of it."

"You tried."

"How do you know that?"

"I—I'm assuming."

"Yes, I tried. But then my eyes . . . or maybe it wasn't my eyes, maybe it just wasn't going well. You have to know when you're defeated. Miriam burned them."

"Excuse me?"

"I asked her to." He laid his head back, blew smoke straight up in the air. "Since then I haven't set foot in the studio."

"I believe you!"

"There's no reason to be sad. Because that's what everything's about: your estimate of your own talent. When I was young and hadn't yet painted anything useful . . . I doubt if you can imagine it. I locked myself up for a week . . ."

"Five days."

"I don't care, five days, to think. I knew that I hadn't yet produced anything that mattered. Nobody can help with stuff like this." He groped for an ash-tray. "I didn't just need a good idea. They're a dime a dozen. I had to find what kind of painter I could become. A way out of mediocrity."

"Out of mediocrity," I repeated.

"Do you know the story of Bodhidarma's pupil?"

"Who?"

"Bodhidarma was an Indian sage in China. Some-body wanted to become his pupil and was turned away. So he followed him. Silent, submissive, year after year. In vain. One day his despair overcame him, he planted himself in Bodhidarma's path and cried, 'Master, I have nothing.' Bodhidarma answered, 'Throw it away!'" Kaminski stubbed out his ciga-rette. "And that's when he found enlightenment."

"I don't get it. If he had nothing left, why . . ."

"During that week I got my first gray hairs. When I went out again, I had the first sketches for the *Reflections*. It was still a long time before the first good picture, but that was no longer the problem." He was silent for a moment. "I'm not one of the greats. I'm not Velázquez or Goya or Rembrandt. But some-times I was pretty good. And that's not nothing. And it was because of those five days."

"I'll quote that."

"You shouldn't quote it, Zollner, you should pay attention to it!" Once again I had the feeling that he could see me. "Everything important has to be reached in sudden leaps."

I signaled to the waiter and asked for the check. Leaps or no leaps, this time I wasn't going to pay for him.

"Excuse me," he said, reached for his stick, and stood up. "No, I can manage." He went past me, taking little steps, bumped into a table, apologized, bumped into the waiter, apologized again, and disappeared into the toilet. The waiter set down the check in front of me.

"Just a moment!" I said.

We waited. The houses increased, their windows reflected the gray of the sky, cars made traffic jams on the street, the rain grew heavier. The waiter said he didn't have all day.

"A moment!"

An airplane rose from the nearby airport and was swallowed by the clouds. The two men at the next table gave me filthy looks and left. Outside I saw the main street, the illuminated sign of a department store, and a fountain despondently dribbling water.

"So?" asked the waiter.

Wordlessly I handed him my credit card. A plane made its blinking descent, more and more tracks started coming together, the waiter returned and said my card was blocked. Not possible, I said, try again. He said he wasn't an idiot. I said I wasn't so sure about that. He stared down at me, rubbed his chin, and said nothing. But the train was already braking and I had no time for an argument. I threw down some cash and grabbed the change. As I was getting to my feet, Kaminski came out of the toilet.

I picked up both bags, mine and the one with his dressing gown, took him by the elbow, and led him to the door. I yanked it open, suppressed the impulse to push him out, jumped down onto the platform, and helped him gently off the train.

"I want to lie down."

"At once. We take the subway and . . ."

"No."

"Why?"

"I've never been on one and I'm not starting now."

"It's not far. A taxi's expensive."

"Not that expensive." He dragged me along the jam-packed platform, avoiding people with remarkable skill; he stepped into the street as if it were the most natural thing in the world, and raised his hand.

A taxi stopped, the driver got out and helped him into the passenger seat. I got in in front, my throat dry with anger, and gave the address.

"Why the rain?" said Kaminski pensively. "It's always raining here. I think it's the ugliest country in the world."

I threw the driver a nervous look. He was fat, with a big mustache, and looked pretty strong.

"Except for Belgium," said Kaminski.

"Were you in Belgium?"

"God forbid. Would you pay? I have no change."

"I thought you had no money at all."

"Exactly."

"I've paid for everything else!"

"Very generous of you. I have to lie down."

We stopped, the driver looked at me, and because I felt awkward, I paid him. I climbed out, the rain lashed my face. Kaminski slid out, I held on to him tight, his stick clattered onto the ground; when I picked it up, it was dripping wet. The marble in the entrance hall bounced the noise of our footsteps back at us, then the elevator whisked us silently upstairs. For a moment I panicked that Elke could have changed the locks. But my key still worked.

I opened the door and listened: not a sound. Two days' worth of mail lay under the mail slot. I coughed loudly, listened again. Nothing. We were alone.

"I don't know if I'm getting this right," said Kaminski, "but I have a feeling that we've found our way into your past, not mine."

I led him to the guest room. The bed was freshly made. "Needs air." I opened the window. "Medicines." I lined them up on the night table. "Pajamas."

"The pajamas are in the suitcase and the suitcase is in the car."

"And the car?"

I didn't reply.

"Ah," he said, "well. Leave me alone."

In the living room my two suitcases were standing, fully packed. So she'd really done it! I went out into the hall and picked up the mail: bills, advertisements, two envelopes addressed to Elke, one from one of her boring friends, the other from a Walter Munzinger. I tore it open and read it, but it was only a customer of her agency, very formal, very correct, must be some other Walter.

There was also some mail for me. More bills, advertisements, *Drink Beer!*, three royalty payments for reprinted articles, two invitations: a book launch next week and an opening tonight, Alonzo Quilling's new collages. Important people would be there. In any normal circumstances I would certainly have been there. A pity nobody knew that Kaminski was here in my apartment.

I stared at the invitation and paced around. Rain exploded against the window. Well, actually, why not? It could change my standing completely.

I opened the larger of the two suitcases and began to sort through my shirts. I would need my best jacket. And different shoes. And, of course, Elke's car keys.

X

"Sebastian. Hello. Come in."

Hochgart clapped me on the shoulder, I punched his upper arm, he looked at me as if we were friends, and I smiled as if I believed it. He was the gallerist here, also sometimes wrote reviews, including some of his own exhibitions, which didn't bother anyone. He wore a leather jacket and had long, straggly hair.

"Can't miss Quilling," I said. "May I introduce you?" I paused for a moment. "Manuel Kaminski."

"A pleasure," said Hochgart and held out his hand; Kaminski, tiny, standing beside me leaning on his stick in his woolly pullover and by now very rumpled corduroys, didn't react. Hochgart froze, then clapped him on the shoulder, Kaminski winced,

Hochgart grinned at me, and disappeared into the crowd.

"And who was that?" Kaminski was rubbing his shoulder.

"Pay no attention to him." Disconcerted, I stared after Hochgart. "He's not important. But there are some interesting pictures."

"And why should I be interested in interesting pictures? You don't mean you've schlepped me to an exhibition? I took a sleeping pill only an hour ago, I'm not sure whether I'm even alive or not, and you bring me here?"

"It's the opening night," I said nervously, and lit a cigarette.

"My last opening was thirty-five years ago and it was at the Guggenheim. Are you out of your mind?"

"Just a couple of minutes." I pushed him along, people saw his stick and his glasses, and made way for him.

"Quilling must really have made it!" cried Eugen Manz, the editor-in-chief of *ArT*-Magazine. "Now even the blind are showing up." He thought for a moment, then said, "Let the blind come unto me," and laughed so hard he had to put his glass down.

"Hello, Eugen," I said carefully. Manz was important; I was hoping for a permanent job on his magazine.

"Let the blind come unto me!" he said again. A slender woman with prominent cheekbones stroked his head as he wiped away his tears and peered at me blearily.

"Sebastian Zollner," I said. "Do you remember?"

"Of course," he said, "I know."

"And this is Manuel Kaminski."

He fixed a watery eye on Kaminski, then on me, then on Kaminski again. "No, seriously?"

I felt a glow. "Of course."

"Oh," he said, and took a step back. A woman behind him let out a yelp.

"Please, what's going on?" said Kaminski.

Eugen Manz went up to Kaminski, bent forward, and held out his hand. "Eugen Manz." Kaminski showed no reaction. "*ArT.*"

"What?" said Kaminski.

"Eugen Manz of *ArT*," said Eugen Manz.

"What's going on?" said Kaminski.

Manz looked at me, disconcerted, still holding his hand out. I waved my arms up and down and rolled my eyes at the ceiling.

"Can't you see I'm blind?" said Kaminski.

"Of course!" said Manz. "I mean, I know. I know everything about you. I'm Eugen Manz of *ArT*."

"Yes," said Kaminski.

Manz decided to withdraw his hand.

"What brings you here?"

"I'd like to know too."

Manz burst out laughing, wiped more tears away, and cried, "This is unbelievable!" Two people with glasses in their hands stood still: the female talking head from one of the TV programs and Alonzo Quilling himself. Last time I'd seen Quilling, he'd had a beard; now he was clean shaven and had a ponytail and glasses.

"Look, everybody!" said Manz. "Manuel Kaminski!"

"What's with him?" asked Quilling.

"He's here," said Manz.

"Who?" said the talking head.

"I don't believe it," said Quilling.

"I'm telling you!" cried Manz. "Mr. Kaminski, this is Alonzo Quilling, and this . . ." he looked blankly at the talking head.

"Verena Mangold," she said hastily. "Are you a painter too?"

Hochgart came up to us and laid his arm around Quilling's shoulders. He jerked back, then remembered this was his gallerist, and let it happen. "Do you like the pictures?"

"Forget the pictures right now," said Manz. Quilling gaped at him. "This is Manuel Kaminski."

"I know," said Hochgart, looking this way and

that. "Has anyone seen Jablonik?" He put his hands in his pockets and left.

"I'm writing a book on Manuel," I said, "which is why we naturally have to . . ."

"I'm an admirer of your early work," said Quilling.

"Really," said Kaminski.

"I have some issues with the later things."

"Is that grass piece in the Tate one of yours?" asked Manz. "It blew me over."

"That's by Freud," said Kaminski.

"Freud?" asked Verena Mangold.

"Lucian Freud."

"My mistake," said Manz. "Mille pardons."

"I want to sit down," said Kaminski.

"The thing is," I said meaningfully, "the two of us are just passing through. I can't say any more."

"Good evening," said a gray-haired man. It was August Walrat, one of the best artists in the country. The connoisseurs all valued him, but he'd never been a success; somehow it had never happened that one of the major magazines had done a piece on him. Now he was too old, and it was just impossible, he'd been around too long and the right moment had passed. He was better than Quilling, everyone knew that. He knew it too, even Quilling knew it. All the same, he'd never get a solo exhibition in Hochgart's gallery.

"This is Manuel Kaminski," said Manz. The thin woman laid her hand on his shoulder and pressed herself against him. He smiled at her.

"But isn't he dead?" said Walrat. The talking head inhaled sharply. Manz let go of the woman. I looked at Kaminski, shocked.

"If I don't sit down soon, that's going to come true."

I took Kaminski by the elbow and led him to one of the chairs lined up against the wall. "I'm writing Manuel's life story!" I said loudly. "That's why we're here. Him and me. Us!"

"Please forgive me," said Walrat. "It's just that you're a classic. Like Duchamp or Brancusi."

"Brancusi?" asked Verena Mangold.

"Marcel was a poseur," said Kaminski. "An imbecile and a showoff."

"Could I interview you some time?" said Manz.

"Yes," I said.

"No," said Kaminski.

I nodded to Manz and held out my hand to say: Just wait, and I'd sort it out. Manz looked baffled.

"Duchamp is important," said Walrat. "You can't just avoid him."

"Importance isn't important," said Kaminski. "Painting is important."

"Is Duchamp here too?" asked Verena Mangold.

Kaminski groaned and let himself down onto a folding chair, and I supported him while Manz bent over my shoulder inquisitively. "You know all about him, yes?" I said quietly.

He nodded. "I wrote his obituary."

"What?"

"Ten years ago, when I was culture editor of the *Evening News*. Stocking up on obituaries was my main job. Thank God that time's over."

Kaminski pulled his stick close to him, his head was sagging and his jaws worked; if there had been less noise, the smacking noise he made would have been audible. Above him, one of Quilling's collages showed a TV set with a thick stream of blood pouring out of it, all spray-painted with the words *Watch It!* Next to it were three of his *Advertisement Papers*: posters from the soap manufacturers DEMOT, onto which Quilling had glued cutouts of figures by Tintoretto. For a time they'd been all the rage, but since DEMOT themselves had started using them as ads, nobody was so sure anymore what to make of them.

Hochgart pushed me aside. "Someone's just let on that you're Manuel Kaminski."

"I told you that already!" I cried.

"I didn't take it in." Hochgart squatted down so that his face was level with Kaminski's. "We must take some photos!"

"Perhaps he could have an exhibition here," the slender woman suggested. Up till now she hadn't uttered a single word. We all stared at her in surprise.

"No, seriously," said Manz, wrapping an arm around her hips. "We must seize the opportunity. Maybe a portrait. In the next edition. Are you still in town tomorrow?"

"I hope not," said Kaminski.

Professor Zabl came wobbling up and tripped over Hochgart, who was still squatting on the floor. "Whatizit?" he said, "whatizit? What?" He'd had too much to drink. He was white-haired, with a lamp tan and, as always, a screaming tie.

"I need a taxi," said Kaminski.

"That's really not necessary," I said, "we're about to leave." I smiled at everyone and explained, "Manuel is tired."

Hochgart got to his feet, dusted off his pants, and said, "This is Manuel Kaminski."

"We'll do an interview tomorrow," said Manz.

"Delighted, I'm sure," said Zabl, advancing shakily on Kaminski. "Zabl, professor of aesthetics." He squeezed between us and sat down on a vacant chair.

"Can we go?" said Kaminski.

A waitress came by with a tray, I took a glass of wine, drank it all in one go, and took another.

"I am, am I not, correctly informed," asked Zabl, "that you are the son of Richard Rieming?"

"Something of the sort," said Kaminski. "Forgive my question, but which paintings of mine are you familiar with?"

Zabl looked at us all, one after the other. His neck trembled. "Just right now . . . at this moment . . . I'll have to pass on that." He exposed his teeth in a grin. "Not basically my thing."

"It's late already," said Manz. "It's not fair to lean on the professor like that."

"Are you a friend of Quilling's?" asked Zabl.

"I wouldn't claim that," said Quilling, "but it's true that I will always see myself as Manuel's pupil."

"Well, you certainly pulled off that surprise," said Manz.

"No," I said, "he's here with me!"

"Mr. Kaminski," said Zabl, "may I invite you to attend my seminar next week?"

"I don't think he's here next week," said Quilling. "Manuel travels a lot."

"Is that a fact?" asked Manz.

"He manages incredibly well," said Quilling. "Sometimes his health worries us, but right now . . ." He touched the dark-stained frame of the *Watch It!* collage. "Knock on wood!"

"Has anyone called for a taxi?" asked Kaminski.

"We're about to leave," I said. The woman with the tray came past again and I took another glass.

"Would ten o'clock tomorrow morning suit you?" said Manz.

"What for?" said Kaminski.

"Our interview."

"No," said Kaminski.

"I'll sort it out with him," I said. Zabl tried to get up, had to grab on to something, and collapsed back onto the chair. Hochgart suddenly had a camera in his hand, and clicked; the flash threw our shadows against the wall.

"Can I call you next week?" I said quietly to Manz. I had to act while he still had some vague memory of the evening.

"Next week's no good." He squeezed his eyes shut. "Week after."

"Great," I said. Across the other side of the room, under three of Quilling's neon tubes glued over with newspaper clippings, I could see Walrat and Verena Mangold standing. She was talking a mile a minute while he leaned against the wall and stared sadly into his glass. I took Kaminski's elbow and helped him to his feet; Quilling immediately did the same from the other side. We led him to the door.

"It's fine," I said, "you can let go!"

"No problem," said Quilling. "No problem."

Manz tapped me on the shoulder, and I let go of Kaminski for a moment. "Let's say the end of this week instead. Friday. Call my secretary."

"Friday," I said, "very good." Manz nodded absentmindedly, the thin lady laid her head on his shoulder. As I turned around, I saw Hochgart in the process of taking a photograph of Quilling and Kaminski. The conversation died away. I hastily grabbed Kaminski's other arm, but too late: Hochgart had finished already. We moved on, the floor felt uneven, and the air seemed to quiver faintly. I'd drunk too much.

We went down the stairs. "Careful, a step!" said Quilling with every tread. I looked at Kaminski's wild hair, his right hand gripped the stick tightly. We got out onto the street. It had stopped raining, and the streetlights were reflected in the puddles.

"Thanks!" I said. "I'm parked over there."

"I'm parked closer," said Quilling. "I can drive him. I also have a guesthouse."

"Don't you have to get back?"

"They can get along without me."

"It's your exhibition."

"This is more important."

"We don't need you anymore!"

"It would be easier my way."

I let go of Kaminski, walked around the pair of them, and said into Quilling's ear, "Let go of him, and get back inside!"

"And who do you think you are?"

"I'm a critic and you have exhibitions. We're the same age. I'm going to be there every time."

"I don't understand."

I went back around and took Kaminski's arm.

"But perhaps I really ought to get back."

"Perhaps."

"It's still my exhibition."

"It is," I said.

"Nothing to be done about it."

"Tough," I said.

"It was a great honor," he said, "a great honor, Manuel."

"And who are you?" asked Kaminski.

"He's just priceless!" cried Quilling. "Good-bye, Sebastian!"

"Good-bye, Alonzo!" For a few seconds we glared at each other furiously, then he turned and ran up the stairs. I led Kaminski across the street to Elke's car. A roomy Mercedes, fast and luxurious, almost as beautiful as the stolen BMW. Sometimes I had the feeling that everyone except me was earning money.

I had to concentrate to stay in the traffic lane, I was a little drunk. I opened the window, the cool air

did me good, I needed to go to sleep soon because tomorrow I was going to need a clear head. The evening had been a real success, they'd all seen me with Kaminski, everything had gone well. Yet suddenly I felt sad.

"I know why you did it," said Kaminski. "I underestimated you."

"What are you talking about?"

"You wanted to show me that I'll be forgotten."

It took me a moment to grasp what he meant. He leaned his head back and let out a deep sigh. "Nobody knew a single picture I'd painted."

"That doesn't mean a thing."

"Doesn't mean a thing?" he repeated. "You want to write about my life. Didn't it bother you?"

"Not at all," I lied. "The book will be terrific, everybody wants to read it. Besides which, you yourself predicted it all: First one's unknown, then one's famous, then one's forgotten again."

"I said that?"

"Absolutely. And Dominik Silva says . . ."

"Don't know him."

"Dominik!"

"Never met him."

"You're not going to tell me . . ."

He snapped off the light and removed his glasses. His eyes were closed. "When I say I've never met

someone, then I mean exactly that. I don't know him. Believe me!"

I didn't reply.

"Do you believe me?" It seemed to be important to him.

"Yes," I said quietly. "Of course I do." And all of a sudden I really did believe it, I was ready to believe anything he said, it didn't matter. It didn't even matter when the book came out. I just wanted to sleep. And I didn't want him to die.

XI

I WAS WALKING down the street. Kaminski wasn't with me, but he was somewhere close and I had to hurry. More and more people were coming toward me. I stumbled, fell to the ground, tried to get up again, couldn't: my body was getting heavier, its weight trapped me there, legs brushed past me, a shoe trod on my hand, but didn't hurt, I used all my strength to stop the ground from crowding against me—then I woke up. It was four-thirty in the morning, I recognized the outlines of the cupboard and the table, the dark window, Elke's bed next to mine, empty.

I pushed back the covers, got up, felt the carpet under my naked feet. A noise of shuffling feet came out of the cupboard. I opened it. Kaminski was sitting inside, huddled up, his chin on his knees, his

arms wrapped around his legs, and he looked at me with bright eyes. He wanted to speak, but with his first words the room dissolved; I felt the weight of the covers on me. A sour taste in my mouth, a dull feeling, headache. Cupboard, table, window, empty bed. Ten past five. I cleared my throat, my voice sounded strange, I got up. I felt the carpet under my feet and looked, shivering, at the checks on my pajamas in the mirror. I went to the door, turned the key, and opened it. "And I thought you'd never ask!" said Manz. "Now do you know?" Jana came into the room behind him. What was I supposed to know? "Oh," said Manz, "stop pretending you're so dumb!" Jana pensively wound a strand of hair around her forefinger. "Waste," said Manz cheerfully, "all folly and waste, my dear." He pulled out a handkerchief, waved at me in an affected way, and laughed so loudly that I woke up. Window, cupboard, table, the empty bed, the tangled covers, my pillows were on the floor, I had a headache. I got up. As I felt the carpet under my feet, I was overcome by such a sense of unreality that I reached for the bedpost, but in one swift movement it eluded my grasp. This time I knew it was a dream. I went to the window and pulled up the blind: the sun was shining, people were walking through the park, cars drove by, it was shortly after ten, and no dream. I went out

into the hall. It smelled of coffee, and I could hear voices in the kitchen.

"Is that you, Zollner?" Kaminski was sitting at the kitchen table in his dressing gown, wearing his dark glasses. In front of him were orange juice, muesli, a bowl of fruit, jam, a basket of fresh baked things, and a steaming coffee cup. Sitting opposite him was Elke.

"You're back?" I said a little uncertainly.

She didn't reply. She was wearing an elegantly tailored suit, and she had a new haircut—shorter, leaving the ears free, softly curling in the nape of her neck. She looked great.

"Horrible dream!" said Kaminski. "A tiny space, no air, and I was locked in, I thought it must be a coffin, but then I realized there were clothes hanging above me and I wanted to paint, but I didn't have any paper. Can you imagine that I dream every night about painting?"

Elke leaned forward and stroked his arm. A childlike smile lit up his face. She threw me a brief glance.

"You've met already!" I said.

"You were also there, Zollner, but that part I don't remember."

Elke poured him more coffee, I pulled up a chair and sat down. "I didn't expect you back so early." I touched her shoulder. "How was your trip?"

She stood up and went out of the room.

"Doesn't look good," said Kaminski.

"Just wait," I said, and went after her.

I caught up with her in the hall, and we went into the living room.

"You had no right to come here!"

"I was in a tough spot. You weren't there, and . . . anyhow, a lot of people would be delighted if I brought them Manuel Kaminski."

"Then you should have brought him to one of them!"

"Elke," I said, reaching for her shoulder, and moving close to her. She looked different, younger, something had happened with her. She glanced up, eyes glistening, a strand of hair fell down over her brow and caught itself in the corner of her mouth. "Let's just forget it!" I said softly. "It's me, Sebastian."

"If you want to seduce me, you should shave. You shouldn't be in your pajamas, and just maybe you shouldn't be sitting beside Rubens waiting to bring him back to the love of his youth."

"Where do you get that from?"

She pushed my arm away. "From him."

"He doesn't talk about it!"

"Maybe not with you. I got the impression he talks about nothing else. I don't suppose you've noticed, but he's really worked up." She looked at

me sharply. "And besides, what kind of an idea is this?"

"It gave me the chance to be alone with him. And I needed the scene for the beginning of the book. Or maybe the end, I have to think about that. That's how I get to know what really happened." For the first time, it felt good to talk to her. "I would never have thought it's so hard. Everyone says something different, almost everything is forgotten, and they all contradict one another. How am I supposed to find out things?"

"Maybe you shouldn't."

"Nothing fits together. He's completely different from the way he was described to me."

"Because he's old, Sebastian."

I rubbed my eyebrows. "You said I still had a chance. What did you mean?"

"Ask him."

"Why him? He's totally senile."

"If that's what you think." She turned away.

"Elke, does it really have to end this way?"

"Yes it does. And it's not tragic, it's not terrible, it's not even sad. Excuse me, I'd like to have broken it to you some easier way. But then I'd never have gotten you out of here."

"That's your last word?"

"I gave you my last word on the telephone. This is

simply superfluous. Order a taxi and go to the station. I'll come back in an hour and I would like the apartment to be empty."

"Elke . . ."

"Otherwise I'll have to call the police."

"And Walter?"

"And Walter," she said, and left the room. I heard her speaking quietly to Kaminski, then the front door closing. I rubbed my eyes, went to the table in the living room, took one of Elke's packs of cigarettes, and wondered if I should try to cry. I lit up, laid the cigarette in the ashtray, and watched it turn to ashes. That made me feel better.

I went back into the kitchen. Kaminski was holding a pencil and a writing pad. His head was tilted against his shoulder and his mouth was open; he looked as if he were dreaming, or listening to someone. It took me a few moments to realize that he was drawing. His hand slid slowly over the paper: his forefinger, ring finger, and little finger were extended, the thumb and third finger were holding the pencil. Without lifting his head, he drew a spiral that broke into little waves here and there, at what seemed to be quite arbitrary points.

"Shall we get going?" he asked.

I sat down beside him. His fingers were contorted, a dense mat of lines was growing in the

middle of the sheet of paper. He made a few swift lines using his wrist, then set the pad aside. Only when I looked again did the mat become a stone and the spirals the circles that this created as it hit smooth water, throwing up spray that suddenly contained the hint of the reflection of a tree.

"That's good," I said.

"Even you can do that." He tore off the sheet of paper, put it in his pocket, and handed me pad and pencil. His hand laid itself on mine. "Imagine something. Something quite simple."

I thought of a house, the way children draw it. Two windows, the roof, the chimney, and a door. Our hands moved. I looked at him: his beak of a nose, his raised eyebrows, I heard the whistling of his breath. I looked back down at the paper. There was the roof already, thinly crosshatched, as if by trails of snow, or ivy, then a wall, a shop window stood open, a tiny figure, formed by three strokes, leaned out, supported on one arm, then the door, it dawned on me that this was an original drawing, if I could just get him to sign it, I could sell it for a lot of money. The door had gone crooked, the second house as well, the pencil slipped down to the bottom corner, something didn't add up anymore; Kaminski let go. "So?"

"It's okay," I said, disappointed.

"Are we driving?"

"Of course."

"Will we take the train again?"

"The train?" I pondered. The car key must still be in my pocket, the car was where I'd parked it yesterday. Elke wouldn't be back for an hour. "No, not today."

XII

I DECIDED to take the highway this time. The man at the tollbooth rejected my credit card. I asked what real job he was running away from, he retorted that I should pay up and get out of his sight, and took the last of my cash. I put my foot on the gas and the power of the engine pressed me gently back against my seat. Kaminski took off his glasses and spat again. A moment later he was asleep.

His chest rose and fell regularly, his mouth hung open, you could see the stubble on his cheeks—neither of us had shaved for two days. He began to snore. I switched on the radio, a jazz pianist was playing riffs, faster and faster, Kaminski snored deeper, I turned up the volume. Good that he was asleep. There'd be no hotel this afternoon, we'd be driving straight back. I would give Elke the car, if she

really insisted on it I'd take my suitcases with me, and I'd bring Kaminski home from there by train. I had everything I needed. The only thing still missing was the central scene, the climactic reencounter with Therese in the presence of his friend and biographer.

I turned off the radio. The dividers streamed toward us, I overtook two trucks, using the slow lane. All that, I thought, was his history. He was the one who'd lived it, now it was coming to an end, and I was no part of it all. His snoring checked itself for a moment, as if he'd read my thoughts. His life. And what about mine? His history. Did I even have one? A Mercedes was driving so slowly that I had to use the shoulder; I honked, pulled back left, and forced him to brake.

"But I have to go somewhere."

Did I say that aloud? I shook my head. But it was true, I did have to go somewhere, and do something. That was the problem. I stubbed out my cigarette. That had always been the problem. The landscape had changed, there were no hills anymore, even the villages and paths were disappearing; it felt as if we were traveling back in time. We left the highway, for some time we were driving through woods: tree trunks and the interlaced shadows of branches. Then there was nothing but sheep meadows.

How long was it since I'd seen the sea? To my own

surprise, I realized I was looking forward to it. I stepped on the gas, somebody honked. Kaminski, startled awake, said something in French and went back to sleep again, a thread of spittle hanging from the corner of his mouth. Houses built of red brick started appearing, and there, suddenly, was the town's name on a sign. A straight-backed woman was crossing the street. I stopped, rolled down the window, and asked for directions. She pointed the way with a movement of her head. Kaminski woke up, got a fit of coughing, gasped for air, wiped his mouth, and said calmly, "Are we there?"

We were driving down the last line of streets in the place. The numbers seemed to be random, I had to drive the length of the street twice before I found the right house. I stopped, and got out. It was windy and cool, and unless I was imagining things, I could smell the sea.

"Have I been here before?" asked Kaminski.

"Not as far as I know."

He pushed his stick against the ground and tried to stand up. He groaned. I went around the car to help him. I had never seen him like this: his mouth was distorted, his brow furrowed, and he looked shell-shocked, almost terrified. I knelt down and fastened his shoes. He licked his lips, pulled out his glasses, and put them on very deliberately.

"Back then, I thought I would die."

I looked at him, astonished.

"And it would have been better that way. Everything else was a lie. Going on, pretending there was still some point to it all. Pretending not to be dead. It was exactly the way she wrote it. She always was smarter."

I opened my bag and groped for the tape recorder.

"This letter was there one day. Just like that."

My thumb found the "record" button and pressed it down.

"The apartment was empty. You've never experienced anything like it."

Would the machine be able to record through the bag? "Why do you think I've never experienced anything like that?"

"You think you have a life. And suddenly, everything's gone. Art means nothing. Everything's an illusion. And you know it and you have to go on."

"Let's go on," I said.

It was a house like its neighbors: two stories, a steep pointed roof, big picture window, a little front garden. The sun was nowhere to be found, veils of cloud covered the sky. Kaminski was breathing hard and I watched him with concern. I rang the bell.

We waited. Kaminski's jaw worked, his hand ran

over the handle of his cane. What if nobody was home? I hadn't thought of that. I rang again.

And again.

A plump elderly gentleman opened the door. He had thick white hair and a lumpy nose, and he wore a shapeless knitted jacket. I looked at Kaminski but he didn't say a word. He stood there bowed, held up by his stick, his head down, and seemed to be listening for something.

"Maybe we have the wrong address," I said. "We're looking for Ms. Lessing."

The fat gentleman didn't reply. He frowned, looked at me, looked at Kaminski, looked at me again, as if he were waiting for some kind of an explanation.

"Does she not live here?" I asked.

"She knows we're coming," said Kaminski.

"Well, not exactly," I said.

Kaminski turned toward me slowly.

"We spoke," I said, "but I'm not sure if I made it clear. I mean . . . basically we agreed to it, but . . ."

"Take me to the car."

"You're not serious!"

"Take me to the car." He had never sounded like that before. I opened my mouth and shut it again.

"Come in, come in!" said the old gentleman. "Friends of Little Therese?"

"Sort of," I said. Little Therese?

"I'm Holm. Little Therese and I are . . . well, we've moved in together. Sharing our twilight years." He laughed. "Little Therese is inside."

Kaminski, attached to my arm, didn't seem to want to move. I pulled him gently toward the door. With every step his stick rapped against the ground.

"Keep going!" said Holm. "And do take your things off!"

I hesitated, but there was nothing to take off. A narrow hall with a brightly colored carpet and a doormat that said "Welcome." Three coat hooks festooned with half a dozen knitted jackets, pairs of shoes lined up on the floor. An oil painting of a sunrise, with a rascally hare hopping over a flowerbed. I pulled out the tape recorder and shoved it unobtrusively into my pocket.

"Follow me!" said Holm and went ahead of us into the living room. "Little Therese, guess what!" He looked back at us. "Sorry, what was the name?"

I waited, but Kaminski said nothing. "This is Manuel Kaminski."

"He knows you from before," said Holm. "Do you remember?"

A bright room with large windows. Flowered curtains, striped rugs, a round dining table, a sideboard with piles of porcelain plates behind the glass doors,

a TV in front of the sofa, an armchair and a coffee table, a telephone on the wall, next to a photograph of an elderly married couple and a reproduction of Botticelli's Birth of Venus. Sitting in the armchair was an old woman. Her face was round, all folds and wrinkles, and her hair was a ball of white. She was wearing a pink wool jacket with a flower embroidered on the front, a checked skirt, and furry slippers. She switched off the TV and looked at us questioningly.

"Little Therese doesn't hear so well," said Holm. "Friends! From the old days! Kaminski! Do you remember?"

She looked up, still smiling, at the ceiling. "Of course." Her hairdo bobbed up and down as she nodded. "From Bruno's firm."

"Kaminski," said Holm loudly.

Kaminski clutched my arm so tightly that it hurt.

"My God," she said. "You?"

"Yes," he said.

For a few seconds there was absolute silence. Her hands, tiny and looking as if they were carved out of wood, brushed over the remote control.

"And I'm Sebastian Zollner, we spoke on the phone. I told you that sooner or later we'd . . ."

"Will you have some cake?"

"What?"

"Have to make coffee first. Do sit down!"

"How kind of you," I said. I tried to lead Kaminski to one of the chairs, but he wouldn't budge.

"I've heard you became famous."

"You predicted it."

"What did I do? God, come on and sit down. It's all so long ago." Without moving a finger, she indicated the empty chairs. I tried once again, Kaminski didn't move an inch.

"So when did you know each other?" asked Holm. "Must be a long time ago, Little Therese never mentioned a thing. She's lived through a lot." She giggled. "It's true, you know, there's no need to blush! Married twice, four children, seven grandchildren. Quite something, don't you think?"

"Yes," I said, "it certainly is."

"You're making me nervous, standing there," she said. "It's so uncomfortable. You don't look good, Miguel, sit down."

"Manuel!"

"Yes, yes, come on, sit down."

With full force I pushed him toward the sofa, he stumbled forward, reached for the arm, let himself down. I sat next to him.

"First a couple of questions," I said. "What I'd like to know from you is . . ."

The telephone rang. She reached for the receiver, said "No!" loudly, and hung up.

"Children from the neighborhood," said Holm. "They call up pretending to be someone else and think we won't notice. But they picked the wrong person!"

"The wrong person." She gave a sharp little laugh. Holm went out. I waited: which of them would start to talk first? Kaminski sat there, bent over, Therese nestled there smiling between the lapels of her jacket; she nodded once, as if some interesting thought had just gone through her head. Holm came back with a tray: plates, forks, a flat, brownish cake. He cut it into slices and gave me a piece. It was dry as dust, hard to chew, and almost impossible to swallow.

"So," I cleared my throat. "What did you do back then, after you left?"

"Left?"

"Left," said Kaminski.

She gave an empty smile.

"All of a sudden you were gone."

"Sounds just like Little Therese," said Holm.

"I took the train," she said slowly, "and headed north. I worked as a secretary. I was very alone. My boss was called Sombach, he always dictated too fast, and I had to correct his spelling. Then I met Uwe—we got married after two months." She looked at the backs of her gnarled hands with their

web of veins. For a moment her smile disappeared and her eyes hardened. "Do you remember that dreadful composer?" I looked at Kaminski, but he didn't seem to know who she was talking about. Her expression softened, the smile came back. "Now you've forgotten the coffee."

"Oops!" said Holm.

"Never mind!" I said.

"He who wants, never gets, and vice versa," he said and stayed sitting.

"We had two children. Maria and Heinrich. But you know them already."

"How would I know them?" asked Kaminski.

"Uwe was in a car accident. Someone hit him head-on, a drunk, he was killed instantly. Didn't suffer."

"That's important," said Kaminski softly.

"The most important. When I heard the news, I thought I was dying too."

"She says that," said Holm, "but she's tough."

"Two years later, I married Bruno. Eva and Lore are his. Lore lives right over there in the next street. You drive straight ahead, third left, then left again. Then you're there."

"Where?" I asked.

"At Lore's." There was silence for a few moments. We looked at one another, confused. "That's where

you said you wanted to go!" The telephone rang, she picked up, cried "No!" and hung up again. Kaminski folded his hands and his stick fell on the floor.

"What business are you in?" asked Holm.

"He's an artist," she said.

"Oh!" Holm's eyebrows shot up.

"He's well known. You shouldn't just read the sports pages in the papers. He was very good."

"That's a long time ago," said Kaminski.

"Those mirrors," she said. "So spooky. The first time you did something that wasn't . . ."

"What annoys me," said Holm, "are those pictures where you can't recognize anything. You don't paint that sort of thing, do you?" Before I could take evasive action, he pushed another slice of cake onto my plate; it almost fell off, and crumbs showered down into my lap. He himself, said Holm, made herbal products: small factory, shower gel, teas, creams for muscle pains. You'd find almost nothing comparable these days, you just had to accept that, a certain decline was built into the order of things. "The order of things!" he cried. "Are you sure you don't want coffee?"

"I've always thought about you," said Kaminski.

"But it's been such a long time," she said.

"I asked myself . . ." He fell silent.

"Yes?"

"Nothing. You're right. It's a long time ago."

"What is?" asked Holm. "You should come out and say it!"

"Do you remember your letter?"

"So what's going on with your eyes?" she asked. "You're an artist. Isn't that a problem?"

"Your letter!"

I bent down, picked up the stick and pushed it into his hand.

"Remember what? I was so young."

"And?"

A thought passed over her face. "I knew nothing."

"You knew more than that."

"That's what I mean," said Holm, "whenever I ask Little Therese . . ."

"Shut up!" I said. He took a long breath and stared at me.

"No, Manuel. I really don't remember anymore." The corners of her mouth turned up, her brow smoothed itself out, and she turned the remote control around and around in her hand without bending her fingers.

"You don't know the best story of all," said Holm. "It was Little Therese's seventy-fifth birthday and everyone was there: her children, the grandchildren, everyone finally together in one place. Nobody was

missing. And when they sang For she's a jolly good fellow, right then, in front of the big cake . . ."

"Seventy-five candles," she said.

"Not that many, there wasn't room. Do you know what she said?"

"There were so!"

"We have to go," said Kaminski.

"Do you know what she said?" The doorbell rang. "Now what?!" Holm stood up and went out into the hall, you could hear him talking quickly and agitatedly with someone.

"Why did you never come?" she asked.

"Dominik said you were dead."

"Dominik?" I said. "You insisted you didn't even know him." He frowned, Therese looked at me in surprise, they both seemed to have forgotten I was there.

"Did he?" she said. "Why?"

Kaminski didn't reply.

"I was young," she said. "One does the oddest things. I was someone else."

"You certainly were."

"You looked different. You were taller and . . . you had such strength. Such energy. If I spent enough time with you, I felt dizzy." She sighed. "Being young is a disease."

"The fever of reason."

"La Rochefoucauld." She laughed softly. Kaminski smiled for a moment, then leaned forward and said something in French.

She smiled. "No, Manuel, not for me. Basically everything started after that."

There was silence for a few moments.

"So what did you say?" he asked hoarsely. "On your birthday?"

"If only I knew!"

Holm came back. "She didn't want to come in, she said she'll wait. Would you like coffee now?"

"It's late already," said Kaminski.

"Very late," I said.

"But you just got here!"

"We could watch TV together," she said. "It's almost time for *Who Wants to Be a Millionaire*."

"Schmidt is a good moderator," said Holm.

"I've read somewhere that he's getting married," she said.

Kaminski leaned over and gave me his hand. I helped him to his feet. I had the impression there was something he still wanted to say; I waited, but nothing came. His hold on my arm was weak, almost imperceptible. In my pocket I could feel the tape recorder, I'd almost forgotten it, still running. I switched it off.

"Are you often in the neighborhood?" asked Holm. "You must come again. Mustn't they, Little Therese?"

"And I'll introduce you to Lore. And her children. Moritz and Lothar. They live in the next street."

"That's nice," said Kaminski.

"What kind of art do you actually do?" asked Holm.

We went out into the hall. Holm opened the front door, I turned around, Therese was following us. "Safe trip, Miguel!" she said, crossing her arms. "Safe trip!"

We went out through the front garden. The street was empty, except for a woman loitering around. I noticed that Kaminski's arm was trembling.

"Drive carefully!" said Holm, and shut the door.

Kaminski stood still and lifted the other hand, the one that held the stick, to his face. "I'm sorry," I said quietly. I couldn't bring myself to look at him. It had turned cold, I closed my jacket. He was leaning heavily on my arm.

"Manuel!" I said.

He didn't reply. The woman turned around and came toward us. She was wearing a black coat and her hair fluttered in the wind. I was so surprised I let go of Kaminski.

"Why didn't you come in?" asked Kaminski. He didn't seem surprised at all.

"He said you were almost finished. I didn't want to prolong things." Miriam looked at me. "And now give me the car keys!"

"Excuse me?"

"I'm taking the car back. I had a long talk on the phone with its owner. I am to tell you that if you make any difficulties, you'll be accused of theft."

"I didn't steal it!"

"The other car, our car, has been located, meanwhile. In the parking lot of a rest stop, with a very polite note of thanks. Do you want it?"

"No!"

She took her father's arm, I opened the door, she helped him into the backseat. He moaned softly, his lips moved but no sound came out. She slammed the door. Nervously I held out the cigarette pack. There was only one left inside.

"I shall allow myself to present you with the bill for my airplane ticket and the taxi fare to get here. I promise you it will not be cheap." The wind whipped through her hair, and her fingernails were chewed down to the quick. The threat didn't bother me. I had nothing left, so she could take nothing away from me.

"I haven't done anything wrong."

"Of course not." She leaned on the car roof. "This is an old man who's been made the ward of his

daughter, right? No one has ever told him that the love of his youth is still alive. You just wanted to help."

I lifted my shoulders. In the car, Kaminski's head was rocking backward and forward, and his lips were moving.

"That's how it is."

"And how do you think I know this address?"

I stared at her, confused.

"I've known it for a long, long time. I visited her already ten years ago. She gave me his letters and I tore them up."

"You *what?*"

"That's what he wanted. We always knew that someone like you would come along."

I took another step back and felt the garden fence on my back.

"He didn't actually want to see her ever again. But after the operation he became sentimental. He asked all of us, me, Bogovic, Clure, everyone he knows. He doesn't know that many people anymore. We wanted to spare him. You must have said something that made him come back to the idea."

"What did you want to spare him? Meeting that silly old woman? And that idiot of a man?"

"That idiot of a man is clever. I assume he tried to save the situation. You don't know how easily

Manuel cries, and how much he enjoys it. You don't know how bad it could have become. And this old woman got free of him a long time ago. She had a life in which he was totally insignificant." She frowned. "Not many people have achieved that."

"He's weak and he's ill. He doesn't manipulate anyone anymore."

"No? When you spoke about a prison, I had to laugh. That's when I knew you were just as much in his hand as the rest of us. Didn't he get you to steal two cars and drive him halfway across Europe?"

I put the cigarette between my lips. "For the last time, I didn't . . ."

"Did he tell you about the contract?"

"What contract"

As she turned her head, for the first time I suddenly saw her resemblance to her father. "I think he's called Behring, Hans . . ."

"Bahring?"

She nodded. "Hans Bahring."

I grabbed the fence. A metal spike stabbed itself into my hand.

"A series of articles in some magazine. About Richard Rieming, Matisse, and postwar Paris. Memories of Picasso, Cocteau, and Giacometti. Manuel talked to him for hours."

I threw away the cigarette unlit, and held tight to the fence, tighter, as tightly as I could.

"Which doesn't mean you rummaged through our house in vain." I let go of the fence, and a thin stream of blood ran over my hand. "Perhaps we should have told you sooner. But you've still got the rest: his childhood, that long time in the mountains. And all his late work."

"He has no late work."

"Right," she said, as if this had just occurred to her. "Then it's going to be a thin book."

I forced myself to breathe calmly. I looked into the car: Kaminski's jaws were working, his hands clasped the stick. "Where are you going now?" My voice sounded as if it were coming from a long way away.

"I'm looking for a hotel," she said. "He's . . ."

"Missed his midday nap."

She nodded. "And tomorrow we're driving back. I'll return the car, then we'll take the train. He . . ."

"Doesn't fly."

She smiled. As I looked back at her, I realized that she envied Therese. That she had never lived a life apart from him, that she too had no history. Just like me. "His medicines are in the glove compartment."

"What happened to you?" she asked. "You look different."

"Different?"

She nodded.

"May I say good-bye to him?"

She stepped back and leaned against the fence. I opened the driver's door. My knees still felt weak, it was good to sit in the car. I closed the door so that she couldn't hear us.

"I want to go to the sea," said Kaminski.

"You talked to Bahring."

"Is that what he's called?"

"You didn't tell me."

"A friendly young man. Very cultivated. Is it important?"

I nodded.

"I want to go to the sea."

"I wanted to say good-bye to you."

"You're not coming with us?"

"I don't think so."

"This will surprise you. But I like you."

I didn't know what to say. It really did surprise me.

"Do you still have the car key?"

"Why?"

His face crumpled, and his nose looked very thin and sharply drawn. "She won't take me to the water."

"And?"

"I've never been to the sea."

"Impossible."

"Never happened when I was a child. Later it didn't interest me. In Nice all I wanted to see was Matisse. I thought I had plenty of time. Now she won't take me. It's my punishment."

I looked over at Miriam. She was leaning on the fence and watching us impatiently. Carefully I pulled the key out of my pocket.

"Are you sure?" I asked.

He nodded. I pushed the "lock" button and all four doors closed themselves with a click. I stuck the key in the ignition and started the engine. Miriam leapt forward and grabbed for the door handle. As we moved forward, she rattled it, as I accelerated she slammed her fist against the window, her lips formed a word I couldn't understand, she ran with us for a few steps, then I could see her in the rear-view mirror, standing there as she let her arms fall and watched us go.

"Move it!" said Kaminski.

The street stretched away, the houses slid past us, already we'd reached the end of the village. Meadows opened up. We were in open country.

"She knows where we're headed," said Kaminski. "She'll get a taxi and follow us."

"Why didn't you say anything about Bahring?"

"It was only about Paris and poor Richard. You get everything else. Surely that's enough."

"No, it's not."

The street headed into a long curve, and in the distance I could see the artificial sweep of a dike.

"Well, you're just going to have to write about someone else," said Kaminski, looking unmoved. "Pity about your big closing scene."

"*Who Wants to Be a Millionaire*," I said. "Bruno and Uwe. Mr. Holm and his herbal products."

"And that sunrise."

He laughed and against my will I laughed too. I replayed it in my head: the living room, the carpets, Holm's chitchat, the old woman's face, the painting in the hall.

I hit the brake, almost choking the engine. "Just a moment. How do you know?"

"About what?"

"You understood me. How did you know about the picture?"

He took off his glasses and turned his head toward me.

"Oh, Sebastian."

XIII

A web of clouds had spun itself across the sky. An umbrella with a broken shaft was stuck in the sand; a hundred yards away from us a boy had just gotten a kite up into the air and was letting out the string. A dock reached out over the water. Kaminski walked cautiously beside me, it was hard for him to keep his balance, with sand sticking to his shoes. Everything smelled of seaweed. The beach was strewn with broken mussels.

"I want to sit down," said Kaminski. He had put on the dressing gown again, the creased material fluttered around him. I held him as he carefully lowered himself to the ground. Then he pulled his legs up and laid the stick down beside him. "Hard to believe. I could have died without ever having been here."

"You're not going to die any time soon."

"Rubbish!" He tipped his head back, the wind tugged at his hair, a big wave slung a shower of spray at us. "I'm going to die soon."

"I have to go back one more time." It was hard to make myself heard over the roar of wind and water. "To get my suitcase."

"Is there anything in it you need?"

I thought. Shirts, pants, underwear and socks, photocopies of my articles, writing stuff and paper, a few books. "I have nothing."

"Then throw it away."

I nodded. Then I stood up and walked out onto the dock. The planks groaned under my feet. Out at the end I stopped, opened my bag, and pulled out my notepad. Page after page, tightly written in my messy scrawl, interleaved with dozens of photocopies from books and old newspapers, and everywhere the letters, underlined in red, M.K. I hesitated for a moment, then let it fall. I thought it would float away slowly, but the water swallowed it at once.

As I went back onto the beach, I reached into the bag and pulled out the camera.

I weighed it in my hand. The entire series of his last paintings. I put my thumb on the buttons that would erase all the pictures from the card.

I hesitated.

My thumb lifted itself again as if of its own volition, and I put away the camera. Tomorrow was another day; time enough to think. I sat down next to Kaminski in the sand.

He reached out his hand. I gave him the car key. "Tell her I'm sorry."

"Which her?"

"Both."

"What will you do now?"

"I don't know."

He raised his head, and for a moment he laid his hand on mine. "That's good, Sebastian."

I stood up and left, the sand crunching under my shoes. As I looked back, Kaminski was stretching his legs. The sky was low and wide. High tide was flooding in.

A NOTE ABOUT THE AUTHOR

Daniel Kehlmann was born in 1975 in Munich, the son of a director and an actress. He attended a Jesuit school in Vienna, traveled widely, and has won several awards for previous novels and short stories, among them the 2005 Candide Award, the 2006 Kleist Award, and the 2008 Thomas Mann Award. His works have been translated into more than forty languages, and his novel *Measuring the World* became an instant best seller in several European countries, selling more than 1.5 million copies. Kehlmann lives in Vienna and Berlin.

A NOTE ABOUT THE TRANSLATOR

Carol Brown Janeway's translations include Bernhard Schlink's *The Reader*, Jan Philipp Reemtsma's *In the Cellar*, Hans-Ulrich Treichel's *Lost*, Zvi Kolitz's *Yosl Rakover Talks to God*, Benjamin Lebert's *Crazy*, Sándor Márai's *Embers*, Yasmina Reza's *Desolation*, and Daniel Kehlmann's *Measuring the World*.

A NOTE ON THE TYPE

The text of this book was set in Monotype Joanna, a typeface designed by Eric Gill, the noted English stone-cutter, typographer, and illustrator. It was released by the Monotype Corporation in 1937. Reflecting Eric Gill's idiosyncratic approach to type design, Joanna has a number of playful features, chief among them the design of the italic companion as a narrow sloped roman.

Composed by Stratford Publishing Services,
Brattleboro, Vermont
Printed and bound by R. R. Donnelley,
Crawfordsville, Indiana
Designed by Wesley Gott